Positively Murder

Netta Newbound

Junction Publishing
New Zealand

Netta Newbound/Junction Publishing
Waihi 3610
New Zealand
nettanewbound@hotmail.com
www.nettanewbound.com

Publisher's Note: This is a work of fiction. Names, characters, places, and incidents are a product of the author's imagination. Locales and public names are sometimes used for atmospheric purposes. Any resemblance to actual people, living or dead, or to businesses, companies, events, institutions, or locales is completely coincidental.

Book Layout & Design ©2013 - BookDesignTemplates.com

Ordering Information:
Quantity sales. Special discounts are available on quantity purchases by corporations, associations, and others. For details, contact the "Special Sales Department" at the email address above.

Positively Murder/ Netta Newbound. -- 1st ed.
ISBN 978-0-473-30819-3

Chapter 1

When I first found out my husband was HIV positive, I returned home, changed into my work clothes and left for my evening shift at the supermarket.

Gavin hadn't said much—what could he possibly say? His stricken grey face told me how devastated he felt.

He'd reached for my hand in the clinic, but I snatched it away, no longer able to look at him, never mind have his dirty rotten paws touch me *ever* again.

I got through the evening on automatic pilot, smiling when necessary, asking the customers about their day, and discussing the weather—the usual chitchat.

But under the surface, my stomach twirled and my head spun.

I hadn't a clue what to expect when I got home. Would Gavin have had the decency to pack his stuff and get the hell out of the house? There would be no denying his infidelity now.

As an insurance salesman, Gavin often stayed away from home. I'd had the odd niggling suspicion he might be up to something over the years, but nothing solid. He'd always been the perfect husband; handsome, funny, attentive and sensitive, as well as an excellent father to our daughters, Yvonne and Stella. On the surface, he portrayed the image of an all-round good guy.

The beeping of the checkout scanner soothed my taut and fragile nerves. The motion of passing each item over the top with a smile on my face calmed me in a strange, yet familiar way.

"Are you all right, chickadee?" Gabby, the store manager, asked as we cashed up for the night.

"Fine." I smiled—aware she would be able to see through my fake grin.

"Are you sure?" She narrowed her twinkling hazel eyes and cocked her head.

"Of course I'm sure, just tired that's all."

Gabby gave an upward nod, and then, with a shrug and another squinty-eyed stare, let it go.

I often walked to work, I enjoyed the exercise. Tonight, every step homeward, through the familiar Surrey streets, tortured me with fear and uncertainty.

Would he have dared to stay? Would I have to throw him out?

The thought of life without Gavin tore my heart to shreds.

Having to face him, to find out all the sordid details of his affair, or indeed affairs, sent adrenaline coursing through my already frazzled veins.

As I rounded the corner, my eyes darted to the space where Gavin always parked his Camry, and my heart sank.

It was empty.

Tremors engulfed my whole body. My legs became heavy and unresponsive and I didn't know if they would carry me the final twenty feet to the front door. Would I fall in a heap to the footpath instead?

All of a sudden, headlights lit up the row of houses in front of me. Gavin's familiar blue vehicle turned the corner and parked.

I inhaled, giving myself a mental shake. The twirling in my stomach made me want to throw up, and I'd never before experienced such a monstrous jangling sensation throughout my whole nervous system.

Gavin stepped from the vehicle and glanced at me sideways, clearly unsure of how I would react. Thirty years together had taught us how to communicate in silence, to read each other's body language and facial expressions to perfection.

"I've been to pick you up," he said. "Gabby said I'd just missed you."

I nodded, digging my keys out of my handbag.

"Melissa?"

I lifted my head and glared at him, deep into his beautiful, vivid blue eyes, and the coward looked away.

I opened the front door and entered the semi-detached, dormer bungalow we'd called home for the best part of twenty-nine years. We'd bought it as new-lyweds, after squirrelling every last penny away until we had enough for a deposit.

Gavin had just started out in sales at the time and Reliance, the insurance company he still worked for, had been good to us over the years. However, working for them meant Gavin had to stay away for part of the month.

To be honest, I always welcomed the break and enjoyed the tales of his travels when he got home. Gavin had the ability to create a fantastic story out of the mundane. In a way, I'd put the success of our marriage down to his frequent excursions.

I kicked off my shoes and hung my jacket on the hook by the door, then slipped into the bathroom, shutting the door behind me.

Once my breathing to return to normal, I unfastened my navy-blue tabard and threw it into the washing basket before using the toilet.

Whilst washing my hands, I scrutinised my reflection in the mirror above the sink.

I didn't look bad for fifty-three years of age. There were a few fine lines, which tripled around my clear, grey eyes when I smiled, but didn't everybody over thirty have them?

Although naturally curvy, I fought hard to keep my body in shape. I never failed to visit my hairdresser at least once a month and although cut short, my white-grey hair shone with health.

Maybe that was the reason.

I'd made the decision to go grey six months ago, after years battling with hair dye. It took me a while to get used to the change and now I preferred it, but maybe Gavin thought it aged me.

I no longer bothered to dress in sophisticated clothing, opting instead for flat shoes, a comfortable t-shirt and leggings. There wasn't much call for power suits and stiletto heels in the supermarket. I knew Gavin worked with some very attractive young women who, by his own admission, were eager to advance their careers in any way necessary. Obviously the temptation had been too great.

I walked through to the kitchen.

Gavin stood at the sink filling the kettle. "I'll make us a coffee, shall I?"

I wanted to launch myself at him, to scratch my nails down his cheeks, tear every last neat and tidy hair out of his neat and tidy head, and scream into his face that I didn't want a damn coffee.

Instead, I said nothing. I fought to control my breathing, and sat at the dining table where we'd solved many a problem over the years.

My legs shook. My breath, so shallow, hardly reached my lungs and I thought I might pass out. Maybe a coffee would do me good. Nothing had passed my lips since lunchtime, and it was now almost 10pm.

Gavin placed two steaming mugs on the table and sat opposite me, his gaunt face another reminder of our predicament.

He'd been out of sorts for weeks, lethargic, and had lost a substantial amount of weight.

Worried out of my mind, I'd made the doctor's appointment. My father had deteriorated in a similar way and he'd been riddled with cancer.

Harold Collins had been our doctor for years; we'd even raised our families together, and we considered him a loyal friend. He gave Gavin a thorough examination, carrying out all the standard health checks for diabetes, cholesterol and heart disease. The initial tests showed up nothing concrete, so Gavin insisted the doctor test for *everything.*

When the first HIV results came back, Doctor Collins explained how, sometimes, other conditions can cross-react to produce a false positive. Then he'd sent more blood to the lab for further testing.

Harold hadn't seemed concerned, so neither was I. When the results came back, the findings floored me.

Thinking about it now, Gavin must have known, especially after the initial test results. He didn't appear shocked—more concerned with *my* reaction.

Harold struggled to meet my gaze when he took my blood, which now needed testing. He'd arranged for us to see an HIV specialist tomorrow afternoon, who would explain the next steps and answer any questions.

Any questions—what a joke. I had one huge, burning question. How the hell does a man, who has been married for thirty odd years, test HIV positive?

I couldn't look at him. All kinds of questions ran through my mind. Had he known? How long had it been going on and with how many women?

We'd never be able to put this right. This wasn't just a case of infidelity, although an affair alone would be enough to rock the most steadfast of marriages. This was HIV! No known cure and no way of turning the clock back.

I knew the basics about HIV. That it's contracted through unprotected sex, sharing needles or blood transfusions and eventually it will develop into AIDS. I'd seen a couple of grim movies which left me emotionally bereft for days afterwards. The girls had been given the obvious lectures over the years but, other than that, I never needed to know more.

I'd never met anybody with HIV or AIDS—would never have wanted to for fear of them contaminating me somehow. Yet here we were, my own husband infected with the deadly virus and a huge probability I'd been infected too.

I raced to the sink and retched. Nothing would come up, but it felt as though a solid lump had lodged in my throat. I struggled to breathe.

I splashed my face with cold water before a rush of hot, salty tears washed down my face.

Suddenly behind me, Gavin pulled me into his arms. "Mel. I'm so sorry, Mel."

I closed my eyes, cherishing the familiar feel and scent of him. I always felt safest in his arms, always thought he'd protect me and the girls with every fibre of his being. Not this. Never this.

The blood pounded in my ears, and with a guttural roar I shoved him backwards, lashing out at him, slapping at his chest and his face.

"Get off me! Get off me!" I screamed. "Leave me alone!"

He grabbed my hands before they could do any real damage, gripping them in his stronger ones, before pulling me to his chest again where he held me tight until all the fight had left me.

My tears subsided and I slid to the cold, terracotta floor tiles.

Gavin joined me and we sat in silence for what seemed like an age, moving only when the pins and needles in my legs forced me to. I got to my feet and walked into the lounge.

Gavin followed soon after and perched on the arm of my chair.

"Mel, I'm sorry. You must be so shocked."

"But not you?" I glared at him. Angry tears pricked my eyes.

He shook his head. "I had my suspicions. Didn't want to admit it, but I've had a niggling doubt for a while now."

"Who is she?"

"Does any of that matter?"

"Are you stupid? Of course it matters. Do you even know?"

He shook his head again. "No."

The tightness in my chest made it even harder to breathe. Hand on my head, I bent forward and balanced my elbow on my knee to stop my hand shaking so much. I took several deep breaths exhaling in controlled blows.

"How long?"

"Mel, I ..."

"How long?" I yelled. "How long have you been making a mockery of me, of our marriage? How long?"

"It's not what you think. I'm not having an affair. I've only ever loved you, had a relationship with you. Mel, you must believe me."

"How long?" I said, through gritted teeth, my voice quieter now.

"On and off, all the time."

"Our entire marriage?" My whole body stiffened. "And I never suspected. How can I be so stupid?" I shook my head, feeling as though my brain might explode.

"It never meant anything—just sex."

"It never meant anything?" I repeated his words, shaking my head. "You might die. *I* might die, and you say it never meant anything!"

"They have medication now. We'll be able to lead a relatively normal life. No one need ever know."

"I'd know. Do you honestly think things can go back the way they were? Carry on as normal? Our marriage, the marriage I've held dear my whole adult life, the marriage that gave me our two beautiful daughters ..." The breath caught in my throat and goose-pimples covered my entire body.

"The girls ...? Oh my God, what if they—?"

"No. It's impossible. The virus needs to be passed with blood."

"But what if you had it before they were born?"

"If I'd been infected twenty odd years ago I would be dead by now. Think about what you're saying for Christ's sake, woman." He got to his feet and strode to the window, shaking his head.

I wasn't sure how long someone could have HIV and still lead a symptom-free life. The thought he'd given my children a death sentence filled me with ab-horrence. I knew I should feel the same about him put-ting my life at risk, but I could cope with that so long as my girls were safe.

"Are you sure?" I asked.

He turned and crouched beside me. "I swear to you, Mel. The girls will not be affected, not directly anyway."

A numb feeling descended over me. "Why, Gavin? I thought we had a good marriage."

He straightened up and sat back on the arm of my chair. "It's nothing to do with our marriage. We've had a perfect marriage."

"Then why? I don't understand," I whispered.

"Why do you think? Sex. Just sex."

"*We* have sex. Okay, maybe not as often as we used to, but still ..."

"We make love, Mel, and it's beautiful, I wouldn't change a thing. But I sometimes need the excitement of straight-out sex with a stranger. I'm able to be totally selfish, as rough as I like, as dirty as I like. I couldn't ask you to do these things. I love you, you're my wife."

I shook my head again, trying hard to understand yet clearly missing the point. "I'd do anything for you— would try at least. I'm not a prude, and who knows I might have even liked it."

"They meant nothing—faceless strangers, nothing more."

"Except they weren't, were they? They were riddled with a deadly virus. Doesn't seem quite so meaning-less when you put it that way, does it? Why didn't you wear a condom?"

"I did." He shrugged. "Sometimes."

I couldn't believe his casual attitude. We could be discussing a shopping list for all the emotion he showed. I leapt to my feet, causing the armchair to tilt.

Gavin tottered and almost fell to the floor, but stead-ied himself just in time.

Standing in the middle of the lounge, my hands pressed to my cheeks, I stared at him. "You make me sick!" I spat the words out. Tears filled my eyes once again. "It's basic self-preservation. Everyone uses condoms nowadays."

"You know why, Melissa." He slid onto the seat I'd vacated. "Don't you remember? I've never been able to perform with a condom on. Oh, and for your information, not everybody uses them."

"Even though the consequences were to catch a sexually transmitted disease and pass it on to me—the woman you profess to love too much to have a bit of dirty sex with." I sneered. "It's funny how you didn't mind infecting me in the process, just because the sex wasn't as enjoyable for you with a condom on. You disgust me."

"I'm sorry. I never thought it would happen to me. I'm choosy. I don't sleep with just anyone."

"Not choosy enough, obviously. You selfish, pathetic little man."

Gavin shuddered as I spoke, apparently shocked by my words. I'd never spoken to him with such venom.

"Calm down, Mel. You know you shouldn't upset yourself like this. You'll make yourself ill again."

"Make *myself* ill again …? You're having a laugh. Are you honestly saying I'm doing this to *myself*? I've been well for years now, but let me make things clear—if I do take a wrong turn, the blame lies solely with you—not me. Got that?" I stormed from the room.

***

Gavin shrugged as his overwrought wife walked out. They had a long way to go before their life could return to normal, but at least he had hope. He figured, while they lived under the same roof, there had to be hope.

Mel hadn't mentioned either of them moving out, which he was grateful about—he knew he deserved all she could throw at him. They'd been together a long time, which must count for something. He still loved her, she meant the world to him—he needed to prove it to her that's all.

Chapter 2

I woke to the shrill peel of Gavin's alarm clock.

He fumbled for the button, muttering expletives.

I closed my eyes, feigning sleep, and stayed that way while he got ready for work. I didn't possess the energy to face him.

I sensed him beside me at one point and braced myself, expecting the usual kiss on the cheek. Instead, he stroked a finger along my jawline before leaving, closing the door quietly behind him.

I had hoped he would go in one of the girls' rooms last night, but instead he'd slipped into bed beside me. I hadn't slept a wink. Gavin dropped off after a couple of hours tossing and turning, but I just lay there, listening to his snores. It felt like we were in the middle of a terrible nightmare.

I shuddered, still bruised and confused after last night's confession.

I'd expected a myriad of excuses. Thought he'd explain what a huge mistake he'd made—an ill-fated one-off, that he'd regretted ever since, blah, blah, blah. That couldn't have been further from the truth.

I needed to get today's appointment out of the way before deciding what on earth I would do about everything. Doctor Collins said the results of my blood tests would be sent to the clinic. But I already knew, in my heart, what they'd tell us.

We still led an active sex life. Maybe less frequent in recent years, but active all the same. That's what confused me more than anything—I'd never turned him away, not once in thirty years.

I dragged myself out of bed and stood under the shower for close on half-an-hour. Although I wasn't working today, Liz, our neighbour, would be around soon for her morning coffee. She came most days and, although I loved her dearly, I couldn't confide in her.

***

At 3pm, Gavin tooted the car horn, and I grabbed my jacket off the hook and met him out at the car.

When we pulled up outside the clinic, I froze, as though glued to the seat by the weight of the dread inside me.

Gavin came round to my side and opened the door.

I hesitated, then picked up my handbag from the foot-well and forced myself from the car, ducking out of the way as Gavin bent to kiss my cheek.

I wished I had brought a scarf or a hat or something to disguise myself. I needn't have worried. There were people from all walks of life in the waiting-room, from a teenage boy to an old woman and lots in between. I figured the clinic must cater for all different illnesses, not just HIV and AIDS. When a young woman entered with a cute baby boy, I prayed the tiny tot hadn't got anything nasty.

Gavin sat on the edge of a plastic seat, chewing at his thumbnail, his knee bouncing up and down. His anxiety showed and although I hated him right now, I desperately wanted to pull him into my arms, to assure him everything would be okay.

A kind-faced, middle-aged woman called our names and I let out an unintentional squeal. I put it down to a reaction of my tightly coiled nerves.

Gavin leapt to his feet. He waited while I picked up my handbag and jacket, then, putting his hand at the small of my back, he guided me behind the woman.

The room she led us to could double as a shoe-box—a table and four chairs almost touched the walls. A small window had been opened but didn't create any relief from the stifling heat.

"Take a seat and Doctor Morgan will be with you in a tick," she said, and then left.

"It's hot in here." I undid the neck of my blouse and fanned myself, feeling claustrophobic.

Gavin jumped up and tried to open the window further, but it had been bolted in place. "Shall I open the door?"

I shook my head. "No, I'll be okay."

Doctor Morgan—a little woman in her thirties, with a head of unruly strawberry blond curls, came into the room. She had a file tucked under her arm.

After all the formalities, she got down to business.

"How are you both?" She glanced from me to Gavin.

We both nodded, giving tentative smiles.

"Now, I want you to feel at ease with me. I'm not going to judge you. I'm here to answer any questions and, believe me, there's nothing I haven't heard a thousand times already—nothing will shock me." She smiled. "Afterwards, I'll advise you where we go from here." She placed the opened the file on the table in front of her.

An awkward silence followed as she read the notes.

"Now, I have had the results of your blood tests, Melissa."

My heart stopped. The room seemed to be getting smaller, and I struggled to breathe.

"The initial tests have returned a positive result."

She waited for her news to sink in.

A riot started in my brain and I couldn't control the tremors that engulfed my body.

"We will send off to the lab for a Western Blot, which is a more definite test. We won't get the results back for a few days, but because you've been exposed to the virus, there is a high chance it will confirm you too, are HIV positive."

"I understand." I nodded, my voice sounding quite civilised considering I wanted to strangle Gavin there and then.

Gavin reached for my hand but stopped. Clearly thinking better of it, he pulled back and sat on his hands instead.

"Would you like me to get you a glass of water? Give you a few minutes alone?"

"No—no thanks, I'll be fine." My voice sounded weak and shaky.

"Now, can you tell me what you already know about HIV?"

Gavin cleared his throat. "I've done some research so I know a bit more than I did. It's an incurable virus that affects the immune system and will develop into AIDS without treatment."

"Yes, that's right. Generally when a person is diagnosed HIV positive, we check their blood count which shows us how advanced the infection is. Can you tell me, Gavin, do you have you any idea when you contracted the virus?"

"No, not really." Gavin exhaled loudly and fidgeted in his seat.

"I'm sorry. These questions are very personal. You *were* asked if you wanted your wife present, weren't you?"

"Yes, I was and I do. She needs to hear all this too."

Doctor Morgan nodded and wrote something down on her notepad. "How many partners do you think you had unprotected sex with in the past say … ten years?"

That had been my question too. I wondered if she'd get more information than I'd been able to.

Gavin shrugged. "I don't know."

She scribbled something down.

"Approximate numbers will do—five?—ten?—more?"

"More."

My head snapped around to look at him and I couldn't help it, but my lip curled in disgust. I didn't care if Dr Morgan could see my sneer.

Gavin wouldn't meet my eyes.

More scribbling.

"Lots more? Twenty? Fifty? Hundreds?" She shrugged. "Thousands?"

I shuddered.

"Hundreds." He glanced at me, his eyes pleading for forgiveness.

My breath caught in my throat. How could this be possible? Hundreds! This nightmare kept getting worse and worse.

"Do you know any of these partners? Would you be able to contact them to inform them they also need to be tested?" The doctor continued.

"No. They were all random."

"I see." More scribbling followed.

"Were these partners men, women or a mixture of both?" She glanced up from her pad giving Gavin an *I'm-sorry-about-this,* smile.

Gavin froze then glanced at me and back to the doctor.

I was puzzled by his hesitation. "Women," I said, glaring at Gavin for confirmation.

Prickles starting at the nape of my neck descended down my entire body and my heartbeat thudded. The truth suddenly dawned on me as I looked into Gavin's tear filled eyes.

"Gavin, tell her." I still scrambled around for some reasonable explanation.

"No, doctor. They were men."

"No!" I cried. "No, that's not true. Tell her, Gavin. That's not true. Please!" I begged him, clawing at his hands.

He gripped my hands in his and fixed his gaze on mine. "It's true, Mel. I'm bisexual."

I gasped and jumped to my feet. Head bowed, my hands clasped my cheeks.

"Melissa, please, hear me out."

I shook my head. "I can't do this." I grabbed my handbag and jacket, hauled on the doorknob and fled through the gap, not waiting for the door to fully open. I had to get away from this new and devastating knowledge.

Gavin walked from the clinic an hour or so later. His usually stiff posture seemed loose, his shoulders slumped, and he dragged his feet as though he had no fight left. His suit jacket hung from his fingertips and trailed on the ground behind him.

I observed him from the bench outside the main doors, and my stomach contracted at his beaten appearance.

He didn't notice me until I called his name. His face lit up.

"I thought you'd gone," he said.

"I did." I shrugged. "Then I came back."

"I'm glad."

We walked to the car in silence.

Half way home I glanced at him. "What did she say?"

"Can I tell you when we get home? I think we both need a brandy."

Gavin never drank in the middle of the day, so I knew to expect even more bad news.

I nodded, conflicting emotions tearing through me. Deep down I didn't want to sympathise—especially after his latest bombshell, but I still cared for this overgrown child. And somehow, the fact that Gavin hadn't slept with other women made things a little easier to stomach, in some sort of twisted logic.

As we turned onto the street, a cry escaped my lips. Our eldest daughter's car was parked on the grass verge in front of the house.

"Oh no! I don't believe it."

"What? What's wrong?" Gavin stared at me.

"I forgot Yvonne and Keith are here to stay for a few days."

Gavin slumped in his seat. "Oh shit." He sighed.

"You go in. I'll run to the supermarket to get something for dinner. We need to act normal. Promise me, Gavin, they can't find out."

"Where should I say we've been? She'll wonder why I'm not at work."

"You'll think of something. You've had enough practice lying over the years."

"Not now, Mel. Please. Not now."

Chapter 3

I arrived home, my arms laden with groceries.

Everyone seemed in good spirits in the lounge. Gavin had turned on the charm and, thank goodness, Yvonne didn't seem the least bit suspicious.

I could breathe again.

Yvonne came through to the kitchen as I put the groceries away.

"So what are your plans while you're here, Vonny?"

She pulled out a stool from the breakfast bar and climbed up. "I'm going with Krystal tomorrow for a dress fitting."

"Ah, yes. I forgot that's what you came for. When is the wedding?"

"Not until July. I told Krystal today, I'm more like an old maid than a bridesmaid. Do you think I'll look silly at my age?" She tossed her golden brown hair dramatically.

I laughed. "How can you be an old maid? You're married."

"You know what I mean. Bridesmaids are usually young."

"Of course not silly, you're gorgeous. Krystal wants to watch out she's not upstaged by you."

Although biased, as every mother is, I wasn't blind and felt certain Yvonne would be the envy of most girls her age. She had a knockout figure, my grey eyes and Gavin's colouring. Her complexion was flawless and her small even teeth gave her cutesy smile a Meg Ryan look.

"You must be joking." She snorted. "Have you seen Krystal lately?"

I shook my head. "No, not since, gosh …" I paused from my chore of stacking the tin cans in the cupboard while I racked my brain. "I think I saw her last at *your* wedding."

"That was five years ago. Well, let me tell you, you won't recognise her. Her hubby-to-be paid for a boob job, a nose job and eye lift. She's got fantastic hair extensions, and she hardly eats anything—she's gorgeous."

"Sounds like it." I curled my lip.

"No honestly, Mum, she is."

"I believe you, but she has always been pretty without all that lot."

"Yeah, but what's wrong with preserving your looks as you get older?"

"Older? Are you kidding me?" I bent to shove a tray of steak into the freezer. "She's only twenty-eight, the same age as you. Want a brew?" I reached for the kettle.

She held up her wine glass. "Dad insisted. Shall I get you a glass?"

I raised a hand, shaking my head. "A bit early for me, thanks."

"I'm on holiday so any time is wine o'clock for me." She giggled.

"Don't be having too much before your dinner." I couldn't help myself, always the nagging mother.

"You want to tell Dad then, he's hitting the brandy."

"Oh, is he now?" I wiped my hands on a tea towel and walked through to the lounge.

Gavin and Keith were engrossed in a discussion about football. They paused mid-sentence when they noticed me standing there.

"Oh hi, love, do you want a brandy?" Gavin jumped up and headed for the drinks cabinet.

"No thanks, I'm having coffee and I think you should too."

"We're all right, aren't we, Keith?"

Keith, ever the lawyer, looked smartly dressed in a pair of formal grey trousers and white shirt. Only the absence of a tie and the open neck of his shirt suggested he might be on holiday. He nodded, a goofy smile on his upturned face.

"Never-the-less, you've had plenty—you'll ruin your dinner," I admonished both of them.

"Nonsense. I fancy a drink and a drink I shall have." Gavin waved his glass in front of him.

I knew there wouldn't be any point arguing. I didn't want to cause a scene in front of our guests. Seething, I fixed a firm smile on my face and glared at Gavin.

I'd almost finished the dinner when Gavin, more upbeat than I'd seen him in ages, rushed through to the kitchen.

"I need another bottle of wine for the table. Did you know your daughter's a lush?" He laughed.

Yvonne appeared behind him. "Hey, cheeky, don't blame me. You keep filling my glass."

He bent over and chose a bottle of wine from the rack before reaching into the top cupboard for glasses. "You don't have to drink it."

Yvonne laughed. "Would be rude not to."

Turning quickly, Gavin collided with the bar stool Yvonne pulled out earlier, and crashed to the floor. The glasses exploded sending shards flying all around the room.

"Gavin! Bloody hell. Calm down for God's sake. You're going to kill yourself," I said.

He sat up—looking a little dazed. Then he lifted his hand up to show me. Blood poured from his palm.

Yvonne reached for a cloth off the sink and grabbed Gavin's hand before I had chance to react.

"No!" I yelled at the top of my voice. "Get away from him. Now!"

Yvonne dropped the cloth and Gavin's hand and stepped back in shock.

"Get out of here. Go on. Get out!" I ushered her forcefully from the kitchen and closed the door.

"Shit, Mel. That was a bit full on," Gavin said.

"You think so, do you? You're spurting contaminated blood all over the place. Do you understand the implications of that?"

"Of course I do, but if you wanted to keep it a secret you have a funny way of going about it."

"So letting you bleed all over our daughter is preferable?"

He shrugged.

"Grow up, Gavin. You know, for an educated man you can be stupid at times."

Once I'd bandaged Gavin's hand, I cleaned up the glass. At least the casserole in the oven wouldn't have any glass in it. We could still eat dinner.

Yvonne popped her head around the door. "Safe to come back in?" She eyed me warily.

"Yeah, course it is, love. I just didn't want you to cut yourself, is all."

I caught the worried glance she sent to Gavin.

"I'm okay, sweetheart. Mum fixed me up."

"Dinner's almost ready," I said. "Vonny do you want to set the table? You'll need to get the best glasses out of the dresser."

"No probs."

She seemed okay again. No doubt a bit confused by my outburst, I'd never screamed at her before. Then again, I'd never been in this kind of situation before.

"Are you up to talking?" Gavin asked, once Yvonne and Keith had gone to bed.

"I guess so." I followed him into the lounge.

He handed me a glass of amber-coloured liquid.

"No, Gavin. I won't drink this."

"You will." He pushed the glass into my hand before pouring another and sitting next to me on the sofa.

"So what's this all about? Bearing in mind, I don't think I can take much more today."

"I wish you hadn't left earlier. You needed to hear first-hand what Doctor Morgan had to say. I'll tell you what I can remember, but you may want to call her in the morning."

"What is it?" I braced myself for more awful news.

"My cell count is very low. I must have been infected for a long time."

"The girls ...?"

"Not that long," he said, impatiently. "But the reason I've been sick and tired all the time is because my immune system is shot."

"Wh-what? What do you mean? You have AIDS?" The words tumbled from my mouth. I couldn't believe he'd spent the past twenty-four hours going on about treatments available that prevent the disease progressing to AIDS.

"Not quite, but apparently the medication is some-times less effective the worse the infection is. My CD4 count is below 300." He took a glug of the brandy, fin-ishing the glass in one. "They're going to start the treatment right away. They need to try to build up my levels, but we just need to prepare ourselves for the worst."

I sipped the brandy. The fiery liquid tasted awful, but I enjoyed the loosening sensation flowing through my body a few moments later.

"What's a CD4 count and what is a normal count?" I took another swig and Gavin topped up my almost empty glass.

"I'm not a hundred percent sure myself. I know they are the cells that fight infection. When the count goes below 200, the virus becomes AIDS. Ideally they like to begin treatment around the 350 mark."

I sipped the brandy again.

"Well, say something."

"What do you want me to say?" He'd been right about one thing, the brandy helped.

Gavin sighed. "We also need to talk about the other issue we discussed today."

"I'd rather not." I didn't have the energy for a fight.

"This needs saying, I'm tired of lies. From now on I promise—no more lies."

"Pity you didn't think to tell me before the appoint-ment, instead of humiliating me in front of the doctor."

"I tried to tell you the other day, but I couldn't."

"How come I didn't suspect a thing? I don't understand." I shook my head.

"I made sure I was careful. That part of my life has nothing to do with us, or home."

"Are you gay?" I'd always been okay with gay until now. Stella, our youngest, was in a lesbian relationship, and although I love her partner Tina, in the back of my mind I hoped the phase would pass.

"No, I'm not gay. I'm bisexual. I'm attracted to both men and women. I know this probably sounds stupid, but I could never be unfaithful to you with another woman."

"What's the difference?" I shrugged. "Man or a woman? The bottom line is you were unfaithful. Do you not get that?"

"To be honest I never thought about it. It was like an itch I had to scratch. I never expected anybody to get hurt."

"You're delusional," I told him. "Gay people don't have a choice, they are what they are. Bisexual is just another word for bloody greedy."

We sat in silence for a while. I thought he had fallen asleep, but when glanced at him, he appeared to be thinking.

"Where do you meet these men?"

"When I stay away I arrange to meet them either in a bar—if I've never met them before, or at my motel room.

I nodded, thankful for his honesty. "And how do you find them?"

"I have an app on my phone. It's a site for married men with bisexual tendencies."

"You mean there's a whole website catering for this kind of thing?" My throat constricted, making my voice high pitched. I swallowed to ease the ache and took another sip.

"Shhhh!" Gavin pointed at the ceiling and Yvonne and Keith's bedroom beyond.

The bungalow had two dormer bedrooms that we'd left set up for the girls.

"God, I must be so naive. I suppose that means there are loads of other unsuspecting women out there just like me?" My stomach turned over.

"I guess." He nodded.

"So now what?"

"What do you mean?"

"Well, you *are* going to stop, aren't you?"

Gavin hesitated for a split second too long and I had my answer before he opened his mouth.

"Yeah," he said.

"Liar! Go to bed, Gavin. You make me sick."

He stood up and left the room.

Once I heard our bedroom door close I allowed tears to fall.

***

Gavin ran his hands through his hair and sat on the edge of the bed.

He'd been making definite inroads with Melissa. She hadn't seemed quite as hostile. Then, not ten minutes after promising no more lies, she'd caught him out with that fucking question.

He'd not even considered whether or not he would still play away. However, she'd taken his hesitation as a lie. And maybe she had a point. The thought of putting an end to his exciting secret life disturbed him more than he cared to admit.

His mobile phone vibrated. He stood and pulled it out of his trouser pocket.

You have 1 new message

He tapped the screen and entered his password. The familiar website opened up, showing a variety of men in various states of undress.

Gavin clicked on the flashing envelope icon.

Looking forward to next week—hope you can still make it. Carl.

Gavin considered cancelling, but what would be the point. He'd met up with Carl on several occasions, and Carl could already be HIV positive for all he knew. Maybe it had been Carl who infected *him* in the first place.

Gavin hit reply.

Sweet, see you then.

A sudden pang of guilt made him think about Melissa. He hated her being an innocent victim in all of this, but she didn't understand his needs.

He'd been a fantastic husband, built a stable and happy life for her and the girls. She'd never wanted for anything. She only took the job in the supermarket because she missed the girls and wanted to get out of the house.

He always made sure nothing upset her for fear of repercussions, and despite her father's misgivings, it had worked for the past twenty-nine years. She still had to take medication every day and have six-monthly check-ups, but other than that, there were no signs of the old problems.

However, he would have to tread very carefully with her now. Her specialist had hammered home the importance of her leading a stress-free life.

Gavin stripped down to his boxers and hopped into bed. He set the alarm clock, then switched off the light, pulling the duvet up to his chin.

The effects of the brandy had begun to wear off, but he felt a throbbing in his boxer shorts. Scratching the tips of his fingers through the silky satin fabric, he groaned. Then he turned on his side, trying to ignore the demands of his pulsating cock.

He usually made use of any random hard-ons with Melissa, but there would be no chance of that tonight or for the foreseeable, come to that.

Not a fan of masturbation—why have a dog and bark yourself had always been his motto—yet he knew he wouldn't get a wink of sleep with the incessant twitching in his pants.

Gavin reached for his phone and searched for images of gay porn. On the rare occasion he searched for anything, it would be for men. Maybe he *was* more gay than straight. He loved Melissa, as a companion, a soul-mate, but he couldn't say he lusted after her.

Pulling the duvet down to the top of his legs, he began to rub his rock hard penis.

When the bedroom door opened, Gavin dropped the phone onto his chest and yanked the duvet up to his chin.

He wasn't fast enough. In the light from the hallway, he saw Melissa shake her head, sneer, then turn and head for the bathroom.

By now, his penis had shrivelled so much it was almost inverted. Gavin pulled his boxers up, placed his phone back on the bedside cabinet and turned onto his side.

Chapter 4

Detective Inspector Adam Stanley couldn't believe it. After all this time, they'd arrested the hit-and-run driver responsible for killing his wife, Sarah.

Not normally an outwardly emotional man, he struggled to blink back the tears. He glanced around the office at everybody racing around, carrying out their duties. All were oblivious of the fact he'd just received the call he'd dreamed about for months.

Matt, his brother-in-law and ex-partner, had told him the basics. He said he would hold off questioning the suspect until Adam arrived, but Adam needed to be quick.

His mind raced. He hadn't been working on anything urgent, nothing that couldn't wait until tomorrow at least. Closing the lid of his laptop, he threw a few more items into his drawer, grabbed his keys, mobile and jacket and headed for the door.

His admin assistant, Calvin, was at his desk.

"Something's come up, Cal. I'll be on my mobile if you need me. Let Frances know, will you?"

"No problem, boss."

Adam glanced at his watch—11.15am. On a good run, a trip from Pinevale, a borough of London, to Manchester took around four hours—give or take. However, he would be hitting the city at the start of rush hour which might be a nightmare. The roads were notorious for being congested, and could delay his arrival by up to two hours. He texted Matt saying he'd left, leaving him to work out the ETA for himself.

After two days of solid rain, the sunshine bounced off puddles on the road. Adam switched on the CD player and sounds of *Adele* began belting from the speakers—his guilty pleasure. It occurred to him that, at long last, his life might be getting back on track.

He pulled up at the station car park at just after five.

Matt jumped up when Adam entered the office, a broad smile on his face, and pulled him into an emotionally charged man-hug.

Adam choked back his emotions for the second time that day.

"Okay, fill me in." Adam slapped Matt on the back and took a step backwards.

"You won't like it, mate." Matt walked back to his desk. "If, like me, you've built up a picture in your head of a terrible monster, you'll be disappointed." He handed a file to Adam.

Adam took a deep, bracing breath before opening the transparent plastic cover.

On the second page, a photograph of Penelope Van Erikson, a frail seventy-three-year-old woman, gazed back at him.

Adam's breath hitched.

"She came in this morning to confess," Matt explained. "Couldn't live with herself any longer."

"Why did she flee the scene?"

"She'd let her driver's license lapse and panicked. She said Sarah and the child darted in front of her and she couldn't stop in time, but we already knew that, didn't we? I thought at least if you met her and talked to her, you'll be able to move on from this—in fact we'll both be able to."

With a pang of guilt, Adam remembered Matt must feel as bad as he did. She had been his sister, after all.

"Thanks, Matt." Adam hesitated. Did he want to go through with this? On the way over he'd rehearsed what he would say, but it no longer seemed relevant. He'd held on to this anger for months. And now, instead of releasing in an almighty explosion, it seemed to be fizzling away to nothing.

His wife had been at work when the accident happened.

She was walking a group of small children to the gym class, when a little girl ran into the road. Sarah managed to push the girl to safety. However, she hadn't been so lucky herself.

The car had killed her instantly. All the witnesses said the driver wasn't at fault, but because they fled the scene, they got the blame for Sarah's death. The fact he couldn't solve something so important almost killed Adam. This had been instrumental in his decision to move to London.

Penelope Van Erikson looked even more frail in person. Adam's heart broke when he noticed how she trembled as they entered the interview room. Her eyes darted from Matt to him as she held her breath; tears brimmed in her large, terrified, green eyes. Her fine, grey hair had been pulled into a bun on the top of her head and reminded Adam of his mum.

They were gentle with her. What would be the point causing her any undue stress? She'd suffered already with the guilt.

Matt charged her, but her only real crime had been failing to stop and report the accident.

Adam didn't think she'd get more than a fine and a ban, and he wouldn't want her to get anything more. It had been an accident, full stop.

While he was in the area, Adam thought he'd better pay his mum a visit. She fussed over him as she always did, thrilled to see her only son. He hugged her before he left and for the third time that day, got a hard lump in his throat. He worried he might be turning into a wuss.

***

I couldn't settle, alternating my position from the sofa to the window to the kitchen table and back again.

Tonight would be the first time Gavin had stayed away from home since this nightmare began. When he phoned earlier, I checked the caller ID then called the number back to get the name of the motel.

I felt guilty for snooping, yet, he deserved nothing less. I searched online for the motel and found it to be self-contained apartments rather than the usual type of hotel where guests have to walk through reception to get to the rooms.

On several occasions, Gavin had argued with his bosses. He didn't want to stay in the accommodation they provided, preferring to choose his own. Now it made perfect sense. A front door of his own meant no interference with any comings and goings during his stay.

My stomach churned. I couldn't shake the nagging thought that he intended to be unfaithful once again.

Paranoia had set in. He wouldn't, would he? Not now he knew the damage he could cause. But I couldn't help myself, mainly because, when we last discussed the situation, he couldn't grasp the severity of it. He didn't care about the people he'd infected, and with a blasé attitude, pointed out that somebody gave it to him in the first place and that *I* had been the only real victim.

We argued, but I couldn't be sure if I'd got through to him. I gave up in the end.

To have any chance of peace, I needed to see for myself. Running into the bedroom, I rummaged around for some dark, inconspicuous clothing. I didn't own anything suitable. I raided Gavin's wardrobe, settling on a pair of rather large sweat pants and top. I found a black cap in the garage that had *Sierra* stitched across the front in gold lettering. I altered the back fitting and placed it snugly onto my head.

In the car, I punched the address into the car's GPS—one hour and twenty-five minutes. Close enough for Gavin to have returned home, if he'd wanted to. I'd be there by seven-thirty. I didn't know what I would do if I found him with someone else.

***

Once he'd joined the M6 heading towards London, Adam hit the loudspeaker and made a call.

"Amanda, it's Adam—Adam Stanley."

"Oh hi, Adam." He could hear the surprise in her voice.

"I'm driving so can't talk long, but I wondered … how do you fancy coming to dinner with me tomorrow night?"

There was silence at the other end of the phone.

"I'm sorry," he said. "Maybe I shouldn't have … no worries."

"No, I—I mean yes, I'd love to," she said.

"Great. I'll pick you up at seven."

As he hung up he knew the time had come to move on. It surprised him how much that final puzzle piece had held him back.

Chapter 5

Carl threw the last of his tools into the back of the van and shut the doors, relieved to have finished work for the day. Today had been gruelling as he'd been working outside in the biting cold, up to his elbows in water. He blew on his fingers to warm them and climbed into the cab.

The cold never bothered him a few years back, but the older he got, the more it seemed to penetrate his bones. At forty-three years of age, he sometimes wished he'd followed a more sophisticated career than that of a plumber. He laughed to himself. Sophisticated? Who was he trying to kid?

He'd never been a suit and tie kind of man. In fact, on the occasions he'd had to wear one—funerals and on his wedding day—he'd looked a right sight. Suits were designed for tall, slender men not short, dumpy ones. Not the type of suit he could afford anyway, and anytime he'd bought a dress shirt, he needed the largest circumference for the neck to fit, which meant the sleeves dangled and the bottom came almost to his knees. Nah, he'd just stick to what he knew.

Pulling up outside his two up, two down in Pinevale, he parked his van half on, half off the curb to allow other vehicles to pass on the narrow street.

Sandy opened the front door—she would have run him a bath—

she knew how cold he got. Not a looker by any stretch of the imagination, her limp, mousy hair hung to her shoulders and her teeth seemed too big for her gaunt face, but she was kind and grateful. His dad had always said, 'make sure your ol' woman's grateful and she'll treat you well.' He'd never uttered a truer sentiment.

They'd been together for seven years now, married for three. He'd done the right thing by her when she got knocked up with Tyson.

He dragged his weary body out of the van and down the path.

"Hi, Carl, I've got your baff ready," Sandy said.

Carl grunted at her as he pushed his way into the small hallway and thrust his bag towards her before heading up the stairs.

Sandy placed the bag down and followed. "I've made a stew for your tea—thought you'd need warming up."

"For fucks sake, woman, let me get through the fuckin' door before you start your incessant chatter."

"Sorry, Carl, I'll get you a drink." She went back downstairs.

Carl heard the brat start to cry. He winced, slamming the bathroom door shut—that's all he needed. A bloke could do with a bit of peace and quiet after the kind of day he'd had.

He stripped off his clothes and slipped into the bubbly water with a sigh.

He heard a sound to the side of him and opened his eyes to see Sandy placing a can of beer on the edge of the bath.

"I don't want that, I'm off out tonight."

"Where to? You dint tell me?" Her face dropped.

"Since when do I tell you everyfing? Somefing's come up, and I won't be having me tea either. Save it for me supper."

Sandy backed out of the room again, taking the beer with her.

Half an hour later, he was dressed in his new jeans, a black t-shirt and brown leather jacket. A pang of guilt, for the way he'd treated Sandy, twisted in his chest.

Downstairs, Tyson sat at the dining table eating fish fingers and beans.

"Hey, bruiser." Carl ruffled his son's hair.

Tyson screamed and pulled away from him. "Naughty Daddy."

Carl laughed.

"Don't do that, Carl, you know he dun't like it."

"All right, keep your hair on." He laughed again. "Sorry about before, San. You know I get grumpy when I'm tired."

"It's okay."

Sandy smiled, but he could tell she still smarted from his earlier treatment.

"Tell you what—let's go to the park on the week-end—feed the ducks."

"I feed the ducks?" Tyson's eyes lit up.

"You sure can." Carl winked.

"That would be nice. It's ages since we've done something as a family." Sandy now smiled.

"That's crap, we always do stuff as a family," Carl snapped.

"You know what I mean. Outside the house and away from the telly."

Carl looked at her sharply, and she cowered away. "Sorry."

"Right, I'm off. I won't be late." He kissed her cheek and grabbed her left tit, squeezing it hard.

Sandy squealed and backed off cupping her breast.

Carl left feeling quite upbeat. He whistled a tune as he walked down the path and jumped into his van.

Twenty minutes later he pulled into the motel carpark. He checked his reflection in his rear view mirror and smiled. Feeling quite pleased with himself, he got out and headed towards the building, and tapped on the door.

***

I parked on the side of the road outside the entrance to the motel.

My stomach churned and I thought I might be sick.

The clocks had changed for British Summer Time on Sunday, and the setting sun created an eerie glow.

A couple of floodlights lit the entrance to the reception and one feeble bulb had been mounted on a post at the end of a long, low building. The apartments themselves had wall lights to the side of the doors.

I skulked through the gate, past reception, sticking to the far fence-line, hidden by the row of shrubs and trees alongside it. There were three vehicles parked up in the numbered spaces. Gavin's blue Camry in number six, a light coloured Nissan in number eight and a white van with Pilkington's Plumbing emblazoned down the side panel parked in the visitor's bay.

The numbers corresponded with the apartments lit up from within. I gathered Gavin must be in apartment six. Doing a full circle of the car park, I kept to the outside edge and with Gavin's dark clothing I thought I'd be invisible if anybody appeared.

I reached the furthest part of the building and like a criminal, silently made my way past the first two apartments, both of which were in darkness.

When I reached number eight, I leaned against the window and listened, barely breathing. The TV blared, but I couldn't hear anything else. After a few minutes, with just the sounds of Coronation Street filling the room, I presumed the occupant must be alone.

I made my way to number six and once again, pinned my ear to the window. At first I heard nothing except faint music then a strange grunting sound. It took me a few moments to recognise the sound.

Horrified, I staggered away from the window almost screaming, and I began to shake uncontrollably. Gavin and a mystery guest were inside having sex.

On wobbly legs, I ran back to the far end of the building and into the bushes, throwing up at the base of a tree.

My head reeled and I needed to sit down. Although hidden from the motel, the chain-link fence didn't hide me from the trucking company next door. On unsteady legs, I made my way back along the fence-line and crouched behind the plumbing van, sitting down on the edge of the concrete.

I had no plan from here. I'd hoped to find that it had been a wasted journey and that I'd hear Gavin snoring away to himself tucked up in his room.

I took a deep breath, needing to control myself while deciding what to do. Something needed to be done to stop Gavin committing this awful crime. But what?

I tried to think rationally, but my brain kept throwing random snippets of information into the mix making me dizzy. I couldn't shake off that disgusting grunting sound.

The dirty rotten bastard couldn't keep it in his trousers even though he knew he would infect anyone he had sex with. He must be sick in the head as well as the body.

There were no other vehicles parked anywhere near the motel except for mine. So I figured the plumber's van must belong to Gavin's guest.

I fished my phone out from the baggy sweat pants pocket and dialled the number on the van.

After several rings, a woman answered.

"Pilkington's Plumbing, Sandy speaking."

I panicked, hung up and vomited once more, this time just missing my feet.

My phone rang with a withheld number. "Hello?" I said, tentatively.

"Hi, I just missed a call from this number. Do you have a plumbing problem?"

Shit! My heart almost stopped along with my breathing. With a spinning head, I found myself saying, "Er-erm. Yes, sorry yes I do. When can you come? I have a leak."

"My husband's left his phone here but he shu'nt be too long. Have you turned your wa'er off?"

"The what, sorry? Oh, the water. Yes, it's off," I said.

A child began to cry in the background.

"Soz about this." Sandy laughed. "Not very professional, is it."

"Oh, don't worry, you go and see to the little one and I'll call back later." I hung up.

So, not only did he have a wife, but a little child too. My blood ran icy cold. These men were animals. This had to stop. I couldn't stand by while more innocent people were harmed. Maybe I couldn't make a difference the world over, but I could make a difference right here, right now.

It may be too late to help the guy in the room, but I'd be damned if I'd allow him to hurt his wife and child.

I skulked back to my car and lay in wait.

Chapter 6

The evening had gone with a bang—literally. Carl laughed to himself, amused by his own joke.

He eased out of the car park, his stomach rumbling. He would be ready for a bowl of stew when he got home. Thinking about home, he felt guilty once again for the way he'd treated Sandy.

He always felt like this when he wasn't with her, vowing to treat her better. But as soon as she opened her big fucking trap she made him want to slap her all over again. He'd swear she did it on purpose.

Not tonight though, he'd pamper her tonight. She had a tough time with Tyson, who was autistic. He was harder to look after than most kids his age.

Carl blamed Sandy's side. Her mum had been a few sandwiches short of a picnic and her brother a schizo. Trust him to marry into a nut-job gene pool.

She did look after him, though. For all her faults, she wasn't a bad wife—never nagging at him, not that she'd get away with it if she tried—and he had more freedom than most married men. Yeah, she wasn't a bad old girl, ugly as fuck, but okay. Plus she had great tits.

He'd get in, have a quick shower and maybe he'd be up to a bit of a cuddle on the sofa, put a smile on the old girl's face.

A movement in the crotch of his jeans made him laugh out loud. His penis never failed him. He rubbed himself as it engorged with blood. Maybe he wouldn't even bother with the shower—bend her over the kitchen sink and give her what for as soon as he got in.

He stepped from the van with one thing on his mind.

Suddenly, a car mounted the pavement behind his van and a short, middle-aged, white-haired woman got out charging towards him. Her finger pointed at his face.

"I know where you've been," she screeched.

"Lady, I've got no idea what you're on about." The woman unnerved him and he took a step backwards bumping into the van.

"Don't give me any of that bullshit. You've been screwing my husband."

Carl's arse almost emptied itself into his jeans.

"Watch your mouth," he hissed. His eyes darted around, making sure no-one overheard the crazy bitch.

"A little more information for you to chow down on. Are you aware he'd riddled with AIDS?"

Shocked, Carl couldn't respond. He tried to absorb what she'd just said, wanted to deny it, shrug her off as a nut case, but he couldn't. He stared at her with his mouth wide open instead.

"I wonder how your poor wife will feel when I tell her you've been putting her life and the life of that little kiddie of yours, in danger.

"Whhooaa ..." How did she know about Sandy and Tyson? He couldn't think straight, but when she turned towards his house and began marching down the path, he lost it.

He leapt forward grabbing her by the shoulder and yanked her back with all his might.

She slammed against the side of the van.

"Listen, lady." Thankfully he'd found his voice. "I haven't a clue what the fuck you're on about, but I suggest you get out of here while you still can."

"I'm going nowhere until I speak to your wife and inform her exactly what she's married to, and that's a promise."

"We'll see about that." Carl grabbed her upper arm and pulled her towards him. Spinning her around he pinned her back against his chest and picked her up bodily. Her legs were kicking like a wild animal, but he wasn't fazed. He rushed her to the back of the van and bundled her inside, slamming the door behind her.

She screamed and the van shook violently. He had no choice but to get her away from there.

He jumped in behind the wheel and sped to a quiet lay-by at the end of the street giving himself a chance to plan his next move.

***

I'd messed up big time, jumping in feet first without a plan. I should have thought about his reaction. Of course, he wouldn't want me to tell his wife his sordid secret.

I intended to wait for Gavin's guest to emerge from the motel room, to make sure he *was* the plumber. However, when he strolled out and got into his van I saw red. Following him had seemed the only logical thing to do. I couldn't allow him to go home and infect his wife.

Now, trapped in the back of his van, the enormity of my actions began to hit me. There would be nothing whatsoever to connect me to this man if I vanished. He could kill me and dispose of my body and that would be the end of it.

I fumbled in my pocket for my phone, realising I'd left it on the dashboard of the car. I needed to keep my head and hatch a plan if I was ever going to escape from this.

Scrambling around in the dark, I tried to find some-thing to defend myself with. My fingers wrapped around a metal shaft, a heavy tool of some kind. I bounced it off my palm a couple of times.

Moments later the van slowed, coming to a complete stop. We hadn't gone very far. I held my breath and waited.

Nothing.

Just as I thought he must have already scarpered, I heard the driver door open and close. Footsteps rounded the back of the van.

I sat, poised, on my bottom with my legs in the air. I'd have one chance to escape, the brute was triple my size. My heartbeat thundered in my ears.

As the door began to open I kicked out with all my might and my abductor flew backwards as the doors hit him with force. I leapt from the van, landing on top of him and striking him repeatedly in the face and head with the tool.

I realised he wasn't fighting back. In fact, he wasn't moving at all. My stomach lurched as I looked at him.

A pool of blood running from underneath his head shone in the light from a nearby lamppost. This didn't make sense. I'd hit him hard, but in the face.

Standing up on shaky legs I couldn't work out what had happened, but one thing I knew with certainty.

This man was stone dead.

Chapter 7

On the final stretch of his journey, Adam's car phone rang. He hit the loudspeaker button.

"Hey, Frances. What's up?"

"Stanley, there's been a homicide in Pinevale—Carl Pilkington—the local plumber. He's had his head bashed in."

"I'm still a good hour away, can you text me the address and I'll meet you there," he said.

Fifty minutes later Adam pulled into Hannah Street, a cul-de-sac in Pinevale.

Adam parked his grey Mondeo on the main road and walked down the narrow, busy little street towards the pandemonium of flashing blue lights.

Despite the late hour, every house had spectators spilling from doorways and upstairs windows.

Adam flashed his ID at the uniformed officer and ducked under the police tape. He rounded the white transit van parked at an angle in a layby backing onto woodland and spied the object of everyone's attention.

A middle aged, Caucasian man lay face up in a pool of blood.

Adam spotted his colleague, Detective Holly Frances, standing by the side of the van, her phone to her ear.

She hung up when she noticed him. Running a hand through her silky brown hair, she sighed, clearly relieved to see him.

"Fill me in, Frances," he said.

"Carl Pilkington—seems to have cracked his head on the edge of the curb. There *is* trauma to his face however, and footprints on the inside of the van doors. Looks as though someone kicked their way out, and crashed the victim to the ground in the process.

"Any idea who?"

"No, nothing yet. Mr Pilkington lived about halfway up the street. His wife said he arrived home around 9pm, before vanishing again.

At around ten-thirty, Charles Brentworth discovered the body while walking his dog."

"Any weapon found? His face is a bit of a mess." Adam bent down to get a closer look.

"Nothing yet. Although somebody's been through the tools in the van. Forensics are onto it and hope to find some fingerprints."

Adam nodded as he straightened up. "Seems like he was up to no good if you ask me. Pulling up here, someone shut up in his van, but he got his just desserts by the look of things."

"Yeah, I agree. Bit of a dodgy character by all account—there have been several domestic incidents over the past few years. The wife never pressed charges though."

"Where is the wife?" Adam asked.

"Sandy Pilkington, lives at number forty-three. She's there now. A neighbour is sitting with her."

"I'll go and have a chat." Adam scooted around the crowd and back underneath the tape.

Sandy Pilkington sat at the window watching the comings and goings, rocking silently.

Adam introduced himself and sat on the edge of the blue leather armchair.

She nodded at him as silent tears ran down her cheeks. She turned back to the window. "Do you know who done it?" she asked, with no emotion in her voice.

"Still early days yet, Mrs Pilkington, but it seems somebody may have been trapped in the van. Would you know anything about that?"

This time she spun around to face him, her eyebrows drawn tight together. "No, that's crazy, who would be in the van?" she cried. "I saw him through the window when he got home and he was smiling as he got outa the van. I went into the kitchen to warm his supper an' ten minutes later he'd gone. All this dun't make sense." She bent and shook her head.

"I know, and I also know the last thing you want to do is answer any more questions, but I have to ask."

She nodded, her bony leg twitching up and down.

"Where had your husband been tonight?"

She shook her head again. "He din't tell me. Just said he was going out and he'd eat when he got home."

"What time did he go out?"

"Not sure. He got home at about six and had a baff. So prob'ly seven or somefing like that."

"Did he often go out at night without you knowing his whereabouts?"

"Now and then. He din't like me questioning him. He said I should train to be one ov you lot." She half smiled, showing a full set of uneven teeth, before her face crumpled and she faced the window again.

Chapter 8

I stumbled through the front door and collapsed in a heap behind it. Only then did I allow the tears to fall.

I had no real memory of getting home. I had been disorientated as I ran away from the van, relieved when I realised we'd gone only about two hundred metres from where I'd parked my car.

When I saw I'd left the driver's door wide open, and the keys in the ignition, I thanked God it hadn't been stolen.

I stopped twice on the hard shoulder of the motorway to vomit, not that I had much to bring up, but I kept dry retching.

I couldn't get the sight of the dead man out of my mind. I couldn't believe my actions had ended with someone losing their life. I had no doubt it would have been me lying there with my skull bashed in if I hadn't done it.

I pulled myself to my feet and walked into the bath-room stripping off Gavin's clothes. As I dropped the sweatpants to the floor, a loud clang made me jump. I reached into the pocket and pulled out the wrench-type tool I'd used to attack my abductor.

Dried blood covered the circular head and once again my stomach lurched. I dropped it to the tiles and threw up in the sink, before splashing cold water onto my face and in my mouth.

After a shower, I wrapped the wrench in a pillow-case and stashed it at the back of the airing cupboard under a pile of bedding and towels. Then I threw Gavin's clothes into the washer on a hot wash cycle before going through to the lounge where I poured my-self a large brandy.

The alcohol didn't seem to have any effect tonight. I paced every room, waiting for the washer to finish be-fore transferring the clothing to the dryer. I wouldn't be able to relax until all the items were washed, folded and back in Gavin's wardrobe.

On one of my many journeys through the house, I noticed the light flashing on the hall phone. I hit the button and the electronic voice informed me one new message had been left at 9.05pm.

"Mel, it's me. Just letting you know I'm off to bed. I can't remember if you're working tonight, so you're probably not even home yet. Anyway, I'll speak to you tomorrow. Goodnight sweetheart. I love you."

I stared at the machine and then deleted the message. How nice for him. He'd had his leg over and then gone off to bed for a good night's sleep, oblivious of the trouble his indiscretion had caused. I was beginning to hate him.

I crawled into bed well after 1am, aching from head to toe. I knew I'd feel even worse in the morning. I guessed it was bruising from the guy throwing me against the side of the van. My neck had stiffened and I couldn't turn to the right without pain shooting through me.

By the time the bright green numbers rolled over to 3am I wanted to scream. Each time sleep came close, I suddenly saw the man's staring eyes, life fading from them and the steady pool of blood spreading beneath his head.

I needed to get away from the visions and memories, but how? I couldn't escape from myself. I slid from the mattress taking the duvet with me and crawled underneath the bed—something I used to do as a child when things got too bad at home. I hadn't done it for years. I hadn't vacuumed under there for a while. It smelled musty and the thought of spiders made me shudder a little, but the closeness of the tiny confined space comforted me somehow. I fell into a strange and fitful sleep.

Startled by the sound of the mailman I jumped up, catching my hair in the springs of the bed. It wasn't as hard to release the strands as it had been as a child—I'd had long hair back then. Now I kept my hair pretty close cropped and I managed to extricate myself without much trouble. I crawled from under the bed feeling quite silly.

After making the bed, I headed to the bathroom. Looking at my reflection in the mirror as I brushed my teeth, I noticed my eyes were dark and puffy. Suddenly my grey eyes were replaced by cold pale blue, dead ones and I screamed and dropped the toothbrush into the sink.

You murdered a man last night. The words came into my head as a thought would, except the calm voice wasn't my own.

Was I going mad like my mum had? She would talk to invisible strangers. After years of battling with depression and bi-polar disorder, she died in a mental hospital when I was nineteen years old. As a teenager, I'd shown signs I might follow in her footsteps, but years of therapy and medication had put an end to that.

But, this morning, I couldn't be sure. My therapist had told me trauma can cause mental illness to re-occur. I didn't feel mad, just in shock. I guess I'd be classed as cuckoo if I didn't feel *anything* after recent events.

I rinsed my toothbrush and wiped down the sink, all the time telling myself to stay calm. Nothing linked me to the dead man. Nobody saw me and as far as anybody knew, I had spent the evening at home, miles away. The only discrepancy with that would be

Gavin's phone call, but I could always say I'd had an early night.

I made myself a coffee and checked the mail. The newspaper headlines made me gasp. My heart stopped.

The article read:

LOCAL PLUMBER KILLED

Police were called to a quiet suburb of Pinevale last night, when a local man was found dead by a neighbour out walking his dog. The dead man's van had been parked in a lay-by bordering a copse of trees notoriously frequented by lovers.

The police hadn't issued a statement by the time we went to print, but sources say they suspect foul play. More details will be released once a post-mortem has been carried out and forensics has completed their search of the area.

I clutched my throat, gasping for air. I knew it would make the news but hadn't expected it quite so soon.

They suspected foul play. I wondered if I'd left anything behind for forensics to find.

I hadn't been wearing the cap when he bundled me into the van. What if I'd left some DNA behind? I knew how it worked, had watched enough CSI. Maybe they were already on their way to arrest me. My legs buckled and I grabbed at the table, lowering myself into a chair, trying to get my thoughts in order.

If you'd left any DNA behind they'd need to test it. That would take a few days. Plus they would need something to match it with. You've not got your DNA on file, so relax.

The strange voice filled my head again, but this time it had a more calming effect on me. I needed to stay focused. Nothing connected me with the dead man, except for my husband's connections to him of course.

I suddenly remembered the call I'd made to the dead man's wife. Fear gripped my core.

Replace the SIM card and you'll be okay.

I hadn't a clue where the voice came from, yet it seemed to have all the answers. The SIM card in my phone had been bought from the supermarket on pre-pay, no contract and nothing to connect me to the number. Only the girls and Gavin called me on it, no one else.

I walked out to the car and found my phone still in the tray of the dashboard. There hadn't been any calls or messages. Taking the back off the phone, I removed the tricky little SIM and dropped it down the drain next to the driveway on the street.

Good girl.

I figured the voice must be the logical part of my brain trying to take control, as the rest of it had gone to absolute mush, and I kind of liked being told what to do.

I glanced at the clock as I walked back through to the kitchen and realised that I needed to be at work in less than an hour. The supermarket was the last place I wanted to be, but I couldn't let Gabby down at such short notice.

Best to keep things as normal as possible.

I nodded. I'd draw less attention to myself that way.

I grabbed a coffee and a slice of toast, changed and headed out the door.

***

I struggled to concentrate during the first part of my shift. In the staff room, while on my break, Gabby moaned about the store owners impending visit. She worried they would make staff cuts like they had at their Leeds and Birmingham stores.

Not in the least interested in Gabby's moans, I flicked through a magazine, letting her waffle on uninterrupted. I was relieved when my break ended so I could get back to the checkout.

Chantelle, a local girl with two young children and no man in her life, stood in my queue when I returned. She was the same age as Stella, though you wouldn't think it to look at them, but they'd been close growing up.

It was common knowledge her parents despaired of the choices she'd made. However, they were both screaming drunks and did very little to help her.

Chantelle rented a flat in a converted Victorian house on the old road. It was no secret she struggled to make ends meet. Rumour had it, when she got desperate, she was known to offer herself to locals for the price of a pint of milk and loaf of bread.

It broke my heart to think of the poor girl having to do such things just to put food in her babies' mouths. I often considered helping her, but Gavin always put his foot down telling me to mind my own business.

Well, Gavin wasn't the boss of me anymore. And now I knew *his* dirty secret, I'd remind him he couldn't judge how people chose to live their lives.

Chantelle stood before me, totting up the cost of the items she had in her basket. Her eyebrows furrowed when she added up the coins in her hand. She didn't have much—a packet of nappies, half a dozen eggs and tray of sausages.

My heart broke for her. The little girl at her side asked her mummy for a chocolate bar.

"No, Brittany, I've got no money, baby," Chantelle said.

I scanned the eggs and sausages and lifted the nappies over to the packing bay without scanning them.

Chantelle looked at me in confusion and I smiled and nodded. She paid me with a handful of coins and I gave her change as if she'd given me a twenty pound note, counting the money out into her hand.

Her eyes bulged as she stared from me to the money then, shoving the cash into her coat pocket, she hurried the little girl through the checkout.

"Oh, Chantelle," I said as she made her way to the door. "You forgot something."

She turned to face me, terror clouding her tired brown eyes.

I handed her a chocolate bar.

Her fingers slowly wrapped around it and our eyes held for a second before she took it from me, smiled and raced from the store.

For a brief moment, I felt immense relief. How nice to be able to make a difference to somebody's life.

I'd always followed the law to the very letter, but where had that got me? I made myself a vow. If I could help another person, then that's what I'd do from now on. Besides, the only people to suffer here were the rich, fat-cat owners who, according to Gabby, were going to rob us of our jobs anyway.

I chuckled to myself. How my life had taken a gi-normous somersault. Goodbye, the meek and mild lit-tle goody-two-shoes, and hello, criminal.

***

I arrived home a little after six. Gavin stood in the kitchen cutting chunks off a block of cheese.

"Hi, love," he said. "I'm making some cheese on toast. Do you want some?"

I shrugged. "Go on then."

In all our married life, I'd never seen Gavin so much as boil an egg. In the past, when working late, I'd have prepared something in the morning and left it in the slow cooker for when he arrived home. However, since this whole mess began, I hadn't cooked a thing, except when Yvonne and Keith stayed.

I left him to it, using the excuse of changing into my pyjamas. The thought of spending the whole evening with him as though nothing had happened filled my throat with a silent scream.

When I returned to the kitchen, Gavin presented me with a plate of chargrilled cheese and a cup of coffee.

"It's a bit burnt, I'm sorry. Just pick the black bits off," he said.

"Thank you." I didn't complain. My eyelids threatened to close from lack of sleep. I took the food gratefully, surprised at my sudden hunger. I hadn't eaten a thing since this morning's toast.

I took the cup and plate through to the lounge and switched on the TV.

Gavin joined me a few minutes later.

"You've had a call from Doctor Morgan. She left a message on the machine."

I shrugged. "I'll call her tomorrow."

I'd avoided several calls from her already, but I couldn't tell Gavin that. I couldn't deal with any more details of the illness right now; self-denial ruled.

If I tried hard enough, I managed to put it out of my mind. I didn't *feel* sick, didn't *look* any different, had no intention of spreading it to anyone, so why worry? I'd deal with it in my own good time.

"So how was your day?" he asked.

"Fine." My eyes were glued to the screen. I might be sitting with him, but drew the line at chitchat. I wanted to scream at him and tell him what his selfish, extra-marital dalliances had turned me into. I wondered what he'd say if I asked him what he'd done last night—if he'd confess. But I knew I couldn't. I had to act as normal as possible and it was going to be a long, hard night.

We ate in silence. Gavin changed the channel to the end of the six o'clock news. The droning voice of the newsreader barely penetrated my distracted thoughts.

Gavin began to choke and his empty plate fell to the carpet. He startled me from my daydream.

An image of the dead man covered the screen. I shuddered, holding my breath.

Stay calm—remember.

I took a deep breath and exhaled slowly.

Gavin, still choking, slammed his chest with the side of his fist, staring at the TV.

The newsreader didn't say much more than the newspaper had this morning.

He stopped choking and picked up his plate.

"What's wrong, Gavin. Did you know him?"

When he didn't respond right away, I thought he might tell me, but he shook his head instead.

"Wha …? Oh no. He just reminded me of someone that's all," he said. He gave a shaky smile.

I nodded, feeling my lip curl as I glared at the lying bastard. Apart from his initial shock, he seemed back in total control. I realised I didn't know this man at all.

Since his choking episode, Gavin had developed an annoying cough. I figured he must have scratched his throat on the burnt toast. My nerves were jangling by 9pm.

Sitting in the same room as him all evening, pretending to watch TV, my performance deserved an Oscar almost as much as his did.

I said goodnight and went to bed. But lay tossing and turning. When Gavin came in two hours later, I stilled and pretended to sleep.

Midnight came and went. Gavin lay at the side of me, sweating like a pig, and his incessant cough drove me insane.

I sat up irritably, unable to take it anymore and I nudged him. The sheets were sopping wet. I'd never seen him sweat like that before. I shuddered. My pyjamas felt damp where we had been touching and it disgusted me.

I got out of bed, unable to stay in there with him like that. I couldn't bear it and not just because of the dank wetness of his skin.

You could always kill him.

I squealed at the suggestion and spun across the room to the window, sitting on the cutesy window seat.

All the houses opposite were in darkness, all except the bedroom light of our good friends Ken and Liz.

They were usually asleep well before now. I hoped they were okay. Liz had been sick of late and hadn't been popping in for her usual morning coffee. I must make an effort to call in on them soon.

More coughing came from Gavin and I walked back to the side of the bed. It *would* make sense to kill him. It would solve a lot of problems. But my heart contracted as I looked at his face. I could see both my daughters in him, Vonny around the eyes and in her colouring, and Stella had his nose and mouth.

This man had been part of every major event in my life. All my memories included him by my side. For all I wished I could strangle him right now for the situation he'd put us in, I knew I couldn't. I was stuck with him whether I liked it or not.

Chapter 9

In his office on the first floor of the police station, Adam sifted through the evidence.

The first twenty-four hours of a murder investigation were the most crucial, but there wasn't much to go on as yet. The initial forensic report confirmed the footprints more than likely belonged to a female, size five—which happened to be the most common women's shoe size in the UK.

All but one partial fingerprint belonged to the victim, but it didn't match anything in the database. No more evidence presented itself at the crime scene.

The medical examiner's report showed the victim had sexual intercourse not long before he died, but then it got confusing. They found semen on his back and inside his rectum, ruling out the mystery woman.

Sandy Pilkington screamed the place down at the suggestion her husband had been having gay sex. Inconsolable, she'd kicked him and Frances out of her house and they could still hear her screams as they drove from the street.

A teenage girl, the Pilkington's next door neighbour, provided one further piece of information. When returning home on Thursday evening, a few minutes late for her 9pm curfew, she'd noticed a light-coloured car parked outside her house. It struck her as odd because the driver's door was wide open and nobody was about.

Adam glanced at the clock and began to tidy his desk. He needed to get home and spruce himself up for his dinner date with Amanda. He didn't think she'd appreciate him turning up in the same clothes he'd worn since 6am, and unshaven to boot.

His stomach did a somersault at the thought of going on a date. Maybe he wasn't ready after all. But there would be no pressure with Amanda.

He'd known her for a few months now. She'd been the prime suspect in a serial homicide enquiry, and Adam had felt an immediate connection to her. He knew she wasn't guilty, even though the evidence and her own husband said otherwise.

It soon came to light her estranged brother, Andrew, had committed the murders. However, Andrew managed to escape capture and still evaded them four months later.

Seven o'clock on the dot, he pulled up outside Amanda's semi-detached house. The curtain twitched in the upstairs bedroom before the light went out.

Moments later, the front door opened as he strode down the path.

"Hi, Adam." Amanda smiled, shyly.

"You look stunning." He held her hand, appraising her up and down before kissing her on the cheek.

He'd only ever seen her in jeans and casual clothing before. Tonight she wore a beautiful, calf length, emerald green dress, deliciously cinched in at the waist, showing her feminine curves off to perfection. Her hair, instead of being tied in a knot on the top of her head, hung loose and shone like spun gold.

She blushed. Standing to the side, she invited him in with a nod of her head.

In the kitchen-dining room, Sandra, Amanda's foster mother, sat on the rug by the fire, reading to Amanda's children, two-year-old Jacob and four-year-old Emma. Mary, Amanda's twelve-year-old niece, lay curled up on the sofa engrossed in some boy band on the TV.

Emma and Jacob got to their feet and ran to him, their arms held out as if he were a long lost friend.

Amanda shrugged into a black jacket and then wrapped a cream-coloured, lace scarf around her neck. "Okay, you lot. Be good for Grandma and straight to bed when she tells you. Are you listening, Em?"

"Yes, Mummy." Emma nodded, her delightful blond curls bouncing.

Amanda bent and kissed each child on the top of the head and turned to leave.

***

Adam had booked a table at his favourite Italian restaurant. Not that he'd eaten in there before, but he'd had plenty of takeaways and could vouch for the food.

The waiter introduced himself as Mario. A tall, slim Italian man in his twenties, he had jet black hair and dark, shifty eyes.

"How original," Adam whispered to Amanda as they followed him to their table, and she giggled.

Mario rushed up behind Amanda and began to slip her jacket off her shoulders.

Adam could tell how uncomfortable she felt. He knew she had issues with strangers getting into her personal space; however, she dealt with it admirably.

Once seated, her shoulders dropped and her hands relaxed in her lap. She tossed her long hair over her shoulder, the strands shone under the lights.

Mario whisked the jacket away and hung it on a coat hook at the back of the room. He then returned and took their wine order. His olive skin perspired in the heat of the room.

Alone again, Amanda cleared her throat. "So how was your week?"

"Great actually. I received some good news on Thursday. They finally found the driver responsible for my wife's death."

"Oh ..." Her eyebrows furrowed.

Reading her face, he realised she hadn't a clue what the hell he was talking about, which was hard to believe considering he knew so much about her.

"Sorry, I thought I'd told you."

She smiled, shaking her head.

"My wife, Sarah, was killed in a hit and run last year. The driver wasn't at fault, but it always haunted me that they took off, without facing the music."

Her eyebrows furrowed again. "I can imagine. It must have been awful."

He picked up his fork and scraped at one of the prongs with his fingernail, before glancing back at her. "An old lady in her seventies handed herself in this week."

"An old lady? Shit! I wasn't expecting you to say that."

"I know. I'd convinced myself it would be a total waste of space, a druggie or alcoholic. Not a terrified grandmother who'd never even had so much as a parking ticket in her life."

"Why didn't she stop? I realise she must have panicked, but even so."

"Her driving licence had lapsed. Stupid really, she'd have saved a lot of heartache if she'd just come forward. She's been going out of her mind with guilt."

"Earlier, you said Thursday—you called *me* on Thursday," she said.

"Yes, that's right. I figured now the final puzzle piece is in place, it's time for me to move on. And here I am." He shrugged, giving her his best knock-em-dead smile.

She laughed. It wasn't the reaction he'd hoped for, which highlighted he needed more practice schmoozing women.

"How's it going with Mary?" he asked.

Mario returned with their wine and made a big production of pouring a splash into Adam's glass, awaiting his verdict before pouring more. He used lots of hand gestures and flicks of a white napkin.

They both burst out laughing once he left them alone again.

"Mary's doing well," Amanda said. "Of course we've had a few wobbly moments here and there, but on the whole she's amazing."

"That's good to hear. Is she settling in at school?"

"Yeah, she's made lots of new friends—she had her first sleepover last weekend."

Amanda's brother left his daughter, Mary, in her care before going on the run. Amanda hadn't even known Mary existed before then, but she'd welcomed her with open arms. Andrew initially vanished at the age of fifteen. For years, Amanda feared their paedophile father, Dennis Kidd, was responsible for his disappearance. When Dennis was released from prison,

Andrew returned, seeking revenge on their childhood abusers one by one.

Adam nodded. "And what about Michael? Do you see much of him?"

"Every second weekend when he takes the kids."

Amanda's husband, Michael, had been having an affair at the same time as the murders. Michael even made a statement pointing the finger at Amanda as the killer. Adam had no time for the man whatsoever.

"And no—I've heard nothing from Andrew," she said.

"I wasn't going to ask that."

"I guessed you'd want to know, and I didn't want the question hanging between us all night."

Adam smiled. "That's not the reason I asked you out, you know."

"I know."

"And anyway, he's vanished, just like last time. I guess he won't be found until he wants to be."

Mario came over to take their order.

"Oh, we haven't even looked at the menus yet." Adam laughed. "Can you give us five more minutes?"

"Certainly, sir." Mario backed away, with a bow and more flicking of the napkin.

"You think he belongs on a stage?" Amanda asked, giggling.

"He's his own one-man show." Adam shook his head in amazement and they both cracked up laughing again as they watched the smarmy young man rush through the kitchen doors.

"What do you fancy?" Adam asked, opening his menu.

"I fancy pasta but my spaghetti sucking skills need a bit of work, especially in this dress." She laughed again and sucked her lips together, twisting them in on each other in an exaggerated kissing motion.

Adam burst out laughing too. "After that little spaghetti sucking display I recommend the lasagne."

"Ha, cheeky!" Her eyes sparkled.

Their relaxed manner in each other's company pleased Adam. He hadn't been sure which way the date would go, considering the amount of baggage they both had.

Chapter 10

I got some sleep by crawling underneath Yvonne's bed, which worried me. It seemed as though my old problem had returned with a vengeance. I hadn't slept *in* a bed for years as a child, but that had been almost thirty-five years ago.

I scrambled out when Gavin called my name, and bumped into him on the stairs leading to the bungalow's two dormer bedrooms.

"Oh, there you are, I've been looking for you. I thought you might be doing an early shift," he said, backing down the stairs.

"No, I'm not working this weekend. I ended up sleeping in Vonny's room because you were soaking wet and wouldn't stop coughing."

"I know. I stripped the sheets off the bed. They're sodden. Maybe the medication I'm taking has side effects, or I could be coming down with something."

"Maybe." I followed him into the kitchen. Gavin's pills were on the worktop, but I hadn't checked them out. Didn't want to know what I had to look forward to.

I couldn't begin to imagine a full weekend in Gavin's company. I wished I'd volunteered myself for the weekend shift.

You need to make a plan.

I screwed up my face and shook my head. A plan? What kind of plan?

I filled the kettle and opened the fridge, disgusted by the meagre contents—two eggs, a sliver of cheese, a squishy, almost rotten tomato and half a loaf. I realised there was one activity I could busy myself with— grocery shopping.

I cooked a cheese and tomato omelette for Gavin and I made do with a slice of toast and coffee.

Afterwards, I took a bath while Gavin caught up with his recorded programmes.

Fresh and ready to face the world, I found Gavin sitting at the kitchen table reading the front page of the paper. He jumped as I entered and opened the newspaper, turning his attention to the centre pages. An image of the dead man now faced me.

The photograph made him appear at least two stone heavier, but there was no mistaking the eyes— cold and lifeless, even before he died. I shuddered, stepping closer to read the article.

My stomach clenched when I read that a woman had been locked in the back of the van. How the hell did they know? My legs turned to jelly and I had to grab the edge of the table in order to keep myself up-right.

Keep calm and pull yourself together.

Gavin, his head still in the paper, didn't appear to notice my reaction.

"I'm going shopping, do you need anything?" I grabbed my keys off the hook and headed for the front door.

"No thanks." His voice sounded thick and gruff.

In the car, I tried to calm my breathing. I was amazed that Gavin hadn't picked up on my strange behaviour. I guess he'd always been self-centered.

You need a plan.

There it was again. I had no idea what type of plan so shrugged it off—the trusted voice had flaws after all.

With a full shopping trolley, I headed to the check-out. Steven, a student who only worked weekends, didn't seem his usual bubbly self.

"Are you okay, Steven?" I asked.

He shrugged. "A bit pissed off, between me and you." He whispered, glancing around.

"Oh?"

"Yeah, Gabby give us all a lecture this morning. She said the till was down last night and she freatened us all wiv our jobs. I don't know why she included me. I haven't even been here since last week."

"I wouldn't worry. She knows it wasn't you. I worked last night. How much is missing?"

"Seventeen quid, give or take."

"Probably just a mistake, these things happen." I gave him my most sincere smile, but inside, my stomach twirled.

I hadn't even thought about the till's balancing when I handed over the cash to Chantelle. I wasn't a very good criminal after all and would have to be more careful in the future. In the larger stores, the operators have to balance their own money trays by the end of their shift, but not in this store. There was a daily float and the tills were used by any available member of staff. I felt guilty for getting the other staff in trouble, but not for what I'd done.

Before heading home, I made a quick stop at the library.

Felicity Carroll had been librarian for the past twenty years or more and had the reputation of being a terrible gossip. She eyed me as I booked a session on the internet.

"Thought you had your own computer at home," she quizzed.

"Internet problems." I smiled.

I chose the computer furthest from Felicity and kept her in my sight at all times. I didn't need her peeping over my shoulder. Satisfied she couldn't see, I typed my question into google.

How to track my partner?

Thousands of sites came up with hundreds of suggestions. I read a few. One woman put her husband's hunting dog collar in the boot of his car and managed to track him, catching him in the arms of his mistress. She humiliated him and threw him out of the house.

Maybe that's all *I* need to do, throw him out. What he did afterwards would be down to him and none of my business.

He won't stop spreading his disease, so you will have to.

I nodded in agreement. Gavin couldn't see any wrong in his continued sexual proclivity.

I glanced back at the screen. Other sites suggested a private detective, which wouldn't work in my case. I already knew what he was up to, I just needed to know when and where.

The top answer was to download an app to his phone. I'd recently taken a *Computers for Beginners* course which enabled me to master how to retrieve my emails and do a google search, but not much else. However, I read each step and felt pretty confident by the time I left the library. First, I would need to upgrade my own phone.

I made a detour to the cell phone shop in the high street.

Half an hour later, I walked out with a snazzy little phone fitted with all the bells and whistles. Finley, the sales assistant, gave me a comprehensive training session. I knew I wouldn't remember it all. However, I had the weekend to master it.

Gavin helped me unload the car and seemed pleased that we finally had some food in the house. It's true what they say—you don't appreciate something until it's gone. Food had never even occurred to Gavin before now. I'm sure he thought the magic pantry fairies stocked the shelves while we slept, never mind helping to carry the bags from the car.

So, although we were behaving civilised in each other's company, things were far from normal. Yet neither of us wished to discuss the problem.

Gavin picked up the mobile phone bag and peered inside, a puzzled look on his face.

"I lost my old phone," I explained. "The salesman talked me into getting a smart-phone, says they're all the rage."

"You should have talked to me. I'd have recommended an IPhone, I love mine."

"This one will do me fine."

Later on, I downloaded the *Find my Phone* app, then the *find my friend's phone* app. I didn't add Gavin's details yet. The website said he would need to allow me access to his whereabouts and would be sent an email for confirmation. I needed to get my hands on his phone before I could go any further.

I didn't have to wait too long. When I went through to the lounge, Gavin had fallen fast asleep on the sofa. I slid his phone off the coffee table and scurried to the bathroom.

Within minutes, I'd downloaded the app onto his phone and hid the icon into a folder I renamed *instruction manual*. I accepted the request when the email arrived before deleting it, and voila—done.

I tiptoed back into the lounge and replaced the phone, then drove to the end of the street.

The app had no problem telling me the whereabouts of Gavin's phone, showing me the address. The map even showed the exact position inside the building.

I whooped with delight.

Chapter 11

The following Tuesday Gavin told me he intended to stay away for the night. I panicked, terrified of what this meant for me.

I tried to talk him out of it, but he looked at me as though I'd gone stark staring mad.

I'd never been bothered in all the years he'd stayed away, and he couldn't understand why I'd make such a song and dance about it now.

"It's my job, Mel." Was all he said before shrugging me off.

After he had left for work, I rang Gabby.

"Sorry to drop you in it, Gabs, but I won't be in to-night." I felt terrible for letting her down but figured she had the whole day to arrange cover.

"What's wrong? Are you sick?"

"You could say that," I said. "I'll explain when I see you." At least I'd have a couple of days to think up a story.

Obsessed with my new gadget, I'd watched every move Gavin made yesterday, although he'd spent most of the day in his office. Today I intended to do the same.

He spent the morning in his office, visiting the village around lunchtime and returning to the office ten minutes later.

At two thirty, he hit the road, heading to London. I figured I should get going myself, giving me plenty of time to plan my next move.

Dressed once again in black, I rummaged in the back of the airing cupboard where I'd hidden the wrench. I couldn't find it.

Where is it? Panic tore at my nerve endings until my hand gripped the pillowcase and I dragged it forward. My legs weakened with relief.

Catching my reflection in the bathroom mirror, I froze.

What the hell am I doing? This is ridiculous. This isn't me.

Stop being a coward. You need to do this.

Over the past couple of days, the voice had changed. Just subtle differences at first, but now I knew exactly who it was.

My mother.

As a child, I'd never argued with my mother. As far as I remembered, no-one else had and come out on top.

"I'm not a coward, but why is all this down to me? I'm a victim too," I said aloud.

If you stand by and allow this to continue, Melissa, then that makes you no better than the snivelling creep you married.

Now get in the car. You *are* doing this, unless you want to be responsible for harming more innocent people.

She was right again, as always. But I couldn't bear the thought of seeing that death stare ever again. Carl Pilkington's eyes haunted me every time I tried to sleep.

What you're doing is the lesser of two evils. Right?

I hesitated and refreshed the app on my phone. It showed Gavin still on the motorway.

I might have known you'd change your mind. You always were a snivelling idiot.

"I'm not a snivelling idiot," I said. "What do you want from me? I'm not a killer. The plumber was an accident."

That's exactly what you are if you allow this to go on. Imagine if your precious Vonny or Stella was married to the disgusting specimen Gavin meets tonight. His wife is someone's daughter JUST LIKE THEM.

He might not be meeting anybody—just because he's staying away.

Have you heard yourself? To tot up figures in the hundreds, he must get his end away every chance he gets. Now pull yourself together, this minute!

I rushed to the sink as fiery bile projected from my stomach, coating my tongue and gums with acrid acid.

Once my stomach settled, I drank a glass of milk to quell the burn.

Of course, everything Mum said was right. What choice *did* I have?

I grabbed my stuff and headed for the car.

***

"Was that the last patient, Denise?" Joe asked as the surgery door closed behind the elderly client.

"Mrs Gillespie was booked in for a filling but she hasn't arrived." Denise shrugged.

"Oh well, that's her hard luck. I'm not waiting around now—she'll have to re-book. You might as well get off, it's almost five anyway. I'll switch the phones over."

Denise didn't need telling twice. She jumped up and snatched her green waxed jacket from the coat stand.

"Thanks, Joe. See you in the morning."

Joe smiled as she almost fell over herself to get out of the door. He thought she liked her job, but he'd never seen anyone more eager to get out of the door eve-ry day.

She'd been his receptionist for three years and he knew no more about her private life today than he had three years ago. Once he made the mistake of trying to question her, and she told him, in no uncertain terms, that it was none of his business.

Although a bit of a dragon, she proved to be fantas-tic at her job. He no longer had unpaid accounts—she told the patients what she expected and nobody ar-gued.

Locking the front door behind her, he watched as she crossed the busy high street and ducked down the side of the building opposite, heading to the multi-storey car park.

Joe glanced at his watch. Five more minutes and he could switch the phones over to the after-hours call centre. He walked behind reception and sat down in Denise's still warm, leather chair.

He pressed a button on the telephone console for an outside line and dialled his home number.

Bethany answered on the first ring. "Helloo-oo."

"Hi gorgeous. How's your day been?"

"Great. Your mum's been here all afternoon. She fed Chloe up on sweets though—I reckon she'll be up all night." She laughed.

"She likes to spoil her only grandchild, what can I say ..."

"I'm just kidding. She seems to love her new home, reckons it's the best place she's ever lived and wishes she and your dad moved into the retirement village years ago."

"They hadn't retired years ago."

"I know. But apparently you can move in there at fifty-five."

Joe shrugged and shook his head. "Anyway, just ringing to remind you I'll be late tonight."

"I remembered. Sonya's gonna call in after work for an hour or two so take your time. It's ages since we've had a catch-up."

"Shall I bring kebabs home for dinner?"

"Oh, that sounds nice—save me cooking."

"Say hi to Sonya for me, if I miss her."

"Will do. Love ya, baby."

"I love you too, darling." He hung up, happier knowing his wife would be occupied for the evening.

He transferred the phones over and walked back into his surgery. After gargling with the pink mouth rinse, he combed his fingers through his stylish brown hair, wrapped a tartan scarf around his neck and shrugged into his navy overcoat.

Opening the top drawer of his equipment cabinet, he pulled out a mobile phone stashed inside. No messages, so he presumed all was still as planned. Switching the phone off he returned it to the drawer. He couldn't use his own phone. Bethany would often search for anything suspicious. She grew up in a family with a serial adulterer for a father, making her hypervigilant to any unusual activity. A spare phone kept his other life separate.

One last glance at his reflection and he headed for the door.

Joe had been a dentist for eight years and had his own practice for five of those. He married Beth six years ago and they had Chloe, the love of his life.

He loved her with an intensity that he hadn't thought possible before she had burst into their world almost four years ago, with her bright red misshapen head, yellow-tinged skin and a set of lungs Dame Kiri Te Kanawa would be proud of. It was love at first sight. Needless to say, she grew into her head and the jaundice cleared, but the lungs she still had. He worried how he would react when she reached the age to start dating. Beth mocked him, saying he'd probably try to lock her in the bell tower. He would, if he could afford to build one on top of their townhouse.

With a twinge of regret, he realised he didn't ask to speak to his daughter, and he wouldn't get to see her until tomorrow now.

At the car, he placed his briefcase into the boot before getting in and heading a few blocks up the road to Green Hill Inn, a converted fun pub. Joe used to frequent the Saturday disco as a teenager. Nowadays the pub got a lot of negative press due to the violence and police presence every weekend. He didn't think there would be much activity on a Tuesday night, though.

The loud music wasn't his thing at all and a headache threatened before he even had a chance to order a drink. At the far end of the bar, the music didn't seem so overbearing.

With a drink in his hand, he took a seat at the back of the lounge, giving him a perfect view of the room.

He didn't have to wait long. Gavin arrived early. Joe recognised him from his profile page and waved a beer mat to get his attention.

Standing up to greet him, they shook hands and exchanged a couple of blokey back slaps.

Joe always hated the first awkward ten minutes or so. He liked what he saw though. Although older than he expected, Gavin had distinguished good looks with an amazing smile and great teeth—an essential feature to Joe.

After a couple of drinks, they'd settled into each other's company and were chatting and exchanging banter as though they'd known each other for years.

By seven o'clock, the bar started filling up with teeny boppers and the horrible clanging music became louder.

"Are you ready to go?" Gavin said.

"Thought you'd never ask." Joe, eager to get out of there, gave his cheekiest smile as he grabbed his coat and scarf from the back of the chair. He felt more relaxed than he had in weeks. In a perfect world, he would live life as a gay man, but he knew he would never have the courage to come out to his family and friends. His parents were staunch Catholics, and he knew the knowledge would probably kill his dad.

And then there was Bethany, his rock. He doubted he'd ever find a better friend. They had a great life with regular sex. Luckily for Beth, he had a great imagination and once his eyes were closed, he could be humping anyone. Often Brad Pitt and Tom Hardy made an appearance.

The guilt of his secret life ate away at him, but Beth suspected nothing and that's the way he intended it to stay.

They walked the few hundred yards to the motel. Gavin opened the door and stood aside, his arm outstretched for Joe to enter.

Joe smiled at him and when Gavin flashed those beautiful teeth, Joe felt his hard-on stir.

***

When I first arrived in the area, the phone app showed me Gavin was in a large, multi-storey office block. I managed to locate his car and parked far enough away he wouldn't notice me, yet still getting a perfect view of his car.

I sat in wait.

Soon after five, Gavin raced from the building.

I followed him to the same motel as last week. He only took minutes to collect his keys and drop his bag off, and then he walked to the pub a few minutes down the road.

I kept a fair distance. Gavin had no reason to suspect I'd follow him, but I couldn't risk him seeing me.

He'd been in the pub for over an hour when I decided to attempt to peek inside. I almost came face to face with Gavin as he walked towards the door, heading straight for me. Thankfully, Gavin's eyes never left the face of his handsome companion. I spun around and held my breath as they passed me by.

Following at a safe distance, I watched as they entered the motel room. I sat in wait on the main road.

Chapter 12

When the tall, dark haired man left the motel and drove to a fast food restaurant. I checked out his car once he'd gone inside.

My heart contracted at the pink, booster cushion on the back seat. I shook my head. How many more innocent people were going to be hurt by these selfish, disgusting creatures?

If I'd been weakening at all, at that exact moment everything changed, as though a switch had been flicked on. I knew what I needed to do.

Deep inside I sensed my mother relax. I had her approval.

***

By eight o'clock, Joe stood in the queue at the local kebab shop. He'd called Beth. Sonya hadn't left yet, so he ordered enough for the three of them.

Grateful for the distraction of Sonya, he would be able to eat his supper and go straight to bed without the third degree Beth subjected him to every time he went out.

He smiled as he thought about his night. When he met men through the website, sex was all they were usually interested in. Sometimes a meeting might be over and done within as little as twenty minutes, from hi to bye.

But he'd enjoyed Gavin's company tonight. They had a lot in common, Joe found himself telling Gavin much too much about his real life.

When Gavin asked to meet up again next week, Joe had jumped at it. He often refused to see a guy more than once, worried that it could cause problems. However in Gavin's case, he made an exception this once.

Like most of the men Joe met, Gavin was married— had been for years. So the last thing he'd want to do is broadcast their meeting to all and sundry. No, this once it should be all right. He could feel it in his water.

As he rounded the corner of his street, Joe pressed a button on his sun visor and the garage door chugged to life, slowly lifting up. He edged his Audi inside, always wary that he might misjudge the narrow space one day and dent his pride and joy.

Once inside, he hit the button again and the door had shut by the time he stepped from the car.

He followed the raucous laughter and found Bethany and Sonya in the kitchen.

"I could hear you both laughing from the end of the street." He smiled as he bundled the stack of kebabs onto the worktop.

"Oh hello, Joe. I didn't hear you come in," Bethany said.

"I'm not surprised!" He kissed his sister-in-law on the cheek, before kissing his wife full on the lips.

"I'll take my food into the lounge and leave you ladies to it." He picked up one of the white paper parcels.

"Oh, Joe, could you do me a favour first? I forgot to take Sabrina out for a widdle. Would you do the honours?" She screwed her face up, comically. "Pretty please?"

"Go on then. But I'm not taking her to the field. As soon as she's done her business we're straight back in."

"That's fine."

Joe unhooked the bright pink dog lead from the back of the kitchen door and called Bethany's pooch from underneath the table.

"Come on, Sabby. You have to make do with me, I'm afraid."

The Bichon Frisé groaned as Joe grabbed her by the collar and clipped on the lead. He yanked on the lead a couple of times before Sabrina lifted her pampered behind from the rug.

"Go with daddy, sweetheart," Beth said in a baby voice she used just for the dog.

Joe shook his head and raised his eyes to the ceiling and Sonya laughed.

***

"Fuck!" I growled as the man drove into a garage. I drove past and parked a little further up the street, then doubled back on foot keeping close to the tree-line, and scooted into the driveway of the three story townhouse.

The garage took up a large section of the front of the house. I peered through the front door. A hallway led to a flight of stairs.

I took a pair of blue surgical gloves, that I'd had the sense to bring with me, from my pocket and pulled them on. Then I opened the side gate, careful not to make a sound.

Steep concrete steps led to the back of the house making the back garden on the same level as the living areas on the second storey of the house.

Female voices came from, what I assumed to be, the kitchen.

I stayed in the shadows, fuming with myself for not acting sooner. I could have dealt with him outside the takeaway, but it didn't occur to me he might park inside a garage.

As I was about to admit defeat, the back door opened and my target shuffled out into the cold night, holding a small dog on a lead.

He walked towards the back of the garden, muttering to the dog that had turned to face me.

***

The temperature had dropped and Joe wished he'd put his scarf back on.

Sabrina whimpered.

"I know, it's cold. So do your thing and we can get back inside," he said.

Sabrina stood stock still and began to shake, still whining.

"Oh, come on, you wimp." Joe laughed. He turned to see what had petrified the stupid dog.

A metal object headed straight for his face.

***

Everything seemed to happen in slow motion. The first blow knocked him onto his back. The second sprayed blood all over the fluffy, white yapping dog. Yet the man continued to scramble backwards towards the house.

My mother's voice calmly urged me on—giving me the courage I needed to finish what I'd started.

It took three more attempts before he stopped moving, but his raspy breathing continued.

One final, well-aimed blow to the centre of his forehead did the trick.

I checked his wrist for a pulse.

Nothing.

The whimpering dog, whose blood-spatter soaked fur reminded me of a comical toy dog, sniffed at her owner.

After one last check of the body, I retraced my steps down the side of the building and back to the car.

I snapped off the gloves and folded them inside each other before driving away.

You're getting good at this.

I smiled, pleased with myself and feeling totally different than I had after Carl Pilkington. This time I was euphoric.

Once home, I went through each methodical step, washing Gavin's clothing. This time I also paid close attention to my shoes and the cap, considering all the blood that had sprayed about.

I rinsed the wrench and placed it in the pillowcase and back into the airing cupboard.

After a long hot shower and a strong cup of coffee, I was sure nobody would ever suspect me of doing a thing.

A strange shift had occurred and I had no remorse for the dead man. In fact, I felt no guilt whatsoever.

That's my girl.

Looking into the mirror, I saw my mum behind my eyes.

"Oh, there you are." I smiled.

Chapter 13

Adam couldn't settle.

He flicked through the television channels, but nothing appealed to him. He tried to read, but couldn't concentrate, and he kept reading the same paragraph over and over.

He considered calling Amanda, but decided not to. A phone call at this hour would freak her out.

Friday night couldn't have gone much better.

A brief, awkward moment when he walked her to her front door had been diffused as Amanda kissed his cheek and gazed into his eyes, thanking him for a wonderful evening.

He'd wanted to skip and click his heels together on his way back to the car; however, he'd never been a dancer and would probably end up face first on the garden path.

His phone rang. "Stanley," he barked into the handset.

"Another homicide," Frances said. "Joseph Edward Bates. A thirty-four-year-old dentist—attacked in the garden of his property this evening whilst walking his dog."

"I'm on my way. What's the address?"

The townhouse was in a well-to-do part of Pinevale.

Frances met him in the front garden and led him around the back and up several steps to the rear of the property.

She told him the victim had popped out for a few minutes with the dog and, when he didn't return, his wife found him with his head stoved in.

The scene was particularly gruesome. The victim looked as though his head had been split with an axe, opening the forehead up in two halves.

"Any weapon?" he asked.

"Nothing yet."

"And I suppose nobody saw anything?"

"Not up to now. It's pretty secluded up here—not overlooked at all. I've called for a team of officers to question the neighbours. Maybe one of them noticed something or *somebody* out of the ordinary."

Adam nodded. "Fill me in on the wife."

Frances checked her notepad. "Bethany Bates, a thirty-two-year-old housewife. They have a young daughter. Nothing much more to tell. We've not been able to question her—she's in shock and pretty out of it."

"Anything else?"

"Her sister was visiting when it happened. They're both inside," she said.

Bethany Bates was disoriented and unable to string a coherent sentence together.

Bethany's sister, Sonya Owens, a pretty redhead with a killer figure, followed him into the kitchen, leaving her sister in the lounge.

"I came to spend a couple of hours with Beth. Joe had gone out for the evening but came back early with takeaways for us all."

"Where had he been?" Adam asked.

"I'm not sure, Beth didn't tell me. He was home no later than 8.30pm. He wasn't drunk, but he's never been a big drinker."

"What happened once he came home? What kind of mood was he in?"

"He was in a great mood, not that I've ever seen him in a bad one, but I remember thinking he was particularly jovial tonight."

"And then?"

She shrugged. "Beth asked him to take the dog out for her. She normally does it herself." Her words came out in a whine as she poked her fingers in the corners of her eyes. "What if … I can't bear thinking if she'd …"

Adam shook his head. "Luckily for her, she didn't, Miss Owens." He patted her arm before continuing. "What type of man was your brother-in-law?"

"Kind, funny, everybody loved him. He's a dentist with his own practice, quite well off, but not flashy. Just down to earth, they both are." She began to cry. "I'm sorry, Detective, but it's a lot to take in."

"That's okay, take your time."

She wiped her eyes with a piece of kitchen roll, smudging mascara down her cheeks, and took several deep breaths. "I'm all right, go on, Detective."

"Did either your sister or her husband have any enemies that you know of? Any feuds or arguments?"

"No, nothing. I don't think I've ever known them to fall out with anybody. Especially Joe. He would always go out of his way to avoid confrontation."

"I see. Well, thank you, Miss Owens. We will need you to come to the station tomorrow, to make a full statement. Your sister too. Maybe she would benefit from a visit from the doctor."

"He's been called. Hopefully, he's on his way."

"That will be all for now, Miss Owens. Thanks for your time."

"I just hope you find whoever did this. Our family will never get over it."

"I can imagine. If you think of anything else in the meantime, please call." He handed her his card.

***

I had gone straight into Vonny's room and crawled under her bed. I didn't need to waste time pretending to sleep in our bed. I'd zonked out until this morning.

Feeling refreshed, I decided to do some much-needed cleaning. I made a start on the kitchen cupboards, cleaning inside, outside and on top, scrubbing with a scouring pad.

Why do you keep your glasses in that cupboard? You should keep all your baking things next to the cooker. The glasses are better off over there.

Although I couldn't see where 'over there' was, I instinctively knew where she meant. I nodded, agreeing with her.

Once the cupboards were cleaned and rearranged to suit my mother, I began all over again in the lounge. I threw out stacks of old magazines that I'd been keeping for goodness knows what. I washed the light shades and skirting boards, and removed all the cushions from the three piece suite, vacuuming underneath.

Your couch is too big along that wall. Why don't you swap it with the chair? At least you wouldn't bump into the arm every time you walk into the room.

I laughed. "I suggested that but Gavin likes to lie on the sofa while watching the TV, without the glare from the window."

Stuff Gavin.

"Yeah, stuff Gavin." I laughed again.

By the time Gavin arrived home, everything had been cleaned and rearranged.

"What's been going on here?" he asked, looking around and a frown on his face.

"Oh, you know—bored. I needed to change some things in my life."

He gazed at me sideways, his right eye squinting, clearly unsure how to respond to my strange mood.

"What's for tea?" he ventured.

"Depends."

"On what?"

"On how adventurous you want to be." I looked at him, unblinking, unsmiling, as I waited for my words to sink in.

"You've not made anything?"

"Got it in one. If you're not in the mood to cook, there's a Chinese menu in the drawer."

He nodded and said nothing. He walked into the kitchen and began banging and clattering about.

"What the hell, Melissa! Where are the fucking mugs?"

I followed him and opened the cupboard above the kettle.

"What's wrong with the mug tree? And where's everything gone from the worktop? It looks stark in here."

"My—I mean, *I'm* sick of clutter. I'm in the process of de-cluttering my life."

Gavin nodded once more, his lips so tightly clamped together they were almost non-existent.

I went back through to the lounge and a few minutes later I heard Gavin ordering food.

I grinned to myself and then sensed my mum chuckling.

Gavin stayed in the bedroom until his meal arrived. I was surprised when he presented me with a plate of sweet and sour chicken, my favourite Chinese food.

A teeny twinge of guilt was soon replaced by the strange numbness that had surrounded me for the past couple of days.

I picked at my food, disinterested, although I hadn't eaten a thing all day.

Gavin turned on the TV and the theme music from the six o'clock news went through my head. The headlines were all about some murdered dentist. When the image of the guy from last night flashed on the screen, I almost fainted. I don't know why, but I hadn't even associated the guy on the news with the one from last night.

The news reader described the dentist as a perfect husband and father. Then his pretty, young wife made an appeal for anybody to come forward who might have any information on his brutal murder.

Although distraught, she was blissfully unaware of the massive favour I'd done her. I could have even saved her life and that of their beautiful little daughter.

See, you did the right thing, Mel. I'm so proud of you.

I glanced at Gavin who seemed in total shock. His eyes were much wider than normal, showing lots of the white, which I didn't like, and his jaw hung loose.

I turned back to the screen, needing to listen to what they were saying, the words seemed to run into each other. I wanted to know if they had any suspects, but I was still none the wiser by the time the story changed to a massive flood somewhere in the Pacific Islands.

Gavin had stopped eating and stabbed his fork into the middle of his food and put the plate on the coffee table. He sat forward in his chair and appeared to be struggling with his breathing.

"Are you not hungry after all?" I asked, knowing full well what was wrong with him. I knew I should feel worse than I did.

"What?" He shook his head, looking at me in confusion.

I nodded at his food.

"Oh no, I'll have it later."

"What's wrong with you? Are you sick?"

Of course, he's sick.

I smiled.

"What's so funny?" Gavin snapped.

"Nothing."

His devastated shock thrilled me a little, I could see him trying to compute how two lovers in two weeks had both turned up dead—brutally murdered.

"So what's wrong with you then?" I pushed.

"Nothing, just indigestion. I'm going to lie down."

The noise from the TV penetrated my brain, similar to white noise. I switched it off.

In the silence, I felt able to relax again. I ate a little more food but had no appetite. After a few minutes, I placed my plate next to Gavin's.

When Gavin came back a few hours later, I hadn't moved a muscle and I was surprised how fast the time had passed.

"What's wrong with you, Mel?" He eyed me strangely.

"Tired. Confused."

"About what?" He reached for my hand and I snatched it away.

"About everything, Gavin. Most of all, about us."

He perched on the edge of his seat, worry filling his beautiful blue eyes. His finger and thumb played at his bottom lip as he stared at his feet. My heart contracted.

Don't go all soft on me now—he's brought it on himself.

"I know but ..."

Gavin's confused expression made me realise I'd spoken aloud.

"... erm, I just wanted to tell you I'm going to move into Vonny's room for a while."

Gavin nodded again. He seemed so sad that part of me wanted to reach out to him, to comfort him, but another part of me wanted to relish in his misery.

Chapter 14

Frances stood in the doorway of his office, her eyebrows tightly knitted and her mouth turned down at the corners.

"What is it?" Adam asked.

"The results of the post-mortem are in and the findings, or lack of them, are worrying." She glanced at the file in her hand. "They confirm Joseph Bates died from his injuries."

"It doesn't take an expert to work that one out." Adam raised his eyebrows and pursed his lips.

"Also confirmed, the weapon used is similar or indeed the same as the one used in the assault on Carl Pilkington—a pipe wrench."

"Shit! So the two murders are connected?" Adam rubbed a hand across his forehead.

"Seems so. Plus, Bates also had sexual intercourse of a homosexual nature not long before his death." Frances slapped the file onto his desk.

"So we have a serial killer on the loose?" Adam pondered the evidence so far.

The results of the DNA testing of the semen found on Carl Pilkington hadn't turned up anything from the database. So, if the second sample was from the same person, they wouldn't be any closer to finding the murderer.

Bethany Bates had made a statement earlier today, but she couldn't shed any light on where her husband had been. He told her he was meeting up with a group of dentists from his college days. They met up often, at least once a month, but she didn't know who they were, or where they went.

"There have been a couple of reported sightings of Joseph Bates in the Green Hill Inn at the time he was supposed to be meeting his dentist buddies," Adam told her. "The witnesses recognised his photo on last night's news."

"Well, at least we have something to go on. Did anyone see who he was with?"

"Both said he'd been in the company of another well-dressed man." Adam rubbed his eyes and sighed. "Other than that, we've got nothing to go on. Zilch. Nada."

"I'm meeting Denise Stubbs, Bates' receptionist, this afternoon. Wanna come along for the ride?" Frances asked.

"Sure, why not. I'm going stir crazy here."

Denise Stubbs unlocked the door when Adam and Frances arrived. She explained her boss had been the only dentist in the practice so there seemed no point in opening up.

Adam liked her. Her no-nonsense attitude amused him.

Although upset by the death of her employer, it became evident early on that she knew nothing of use to them. They had worked together for a long time, but their relationship had been purely professional.

"Do you mind if we take a look around?" Adam asked.

"Knock yourself out," Denise said. Her shrug caused her straight brown hair to shimmy. She didn't strike Adam as the type of person to spend hours grooming herself, but her immaculate bob said otherwise.

The surgery held no clues of Joseph Bates the man. It was no different from any other dental surgery he'd visited in his lifetime—the smell made him shudder. He hated dentists.

"So what now?" Denise asked as they stepped back into the reception area.

"In what way, Ms Stubbs?"

"I've obviously lost my job, but will I get any extra pay to tide me over. I've got two young kiddies at home and a useless drunk of a husband."

"That's nothing to do with us I'm afraid. But I'm sure there'll be something to protect you in this case. You would've signed a contract, I presume?" Adam said.

Denise nodded.

"It should tell you what length of notice you're entitled to."

"Oh yeah, I never thought of that."

"Thanks for making time to meet us, Ms Stubbs. And good luck for the future."

"You're a nice guy for a DI, aren't you, sir?" Frances said as they approached the car.

"I'd appreciate it if you kept that gold nugget to yourself, Frances." He laughed.

***

I called in sick for Gavin the next morning.

He refused to get out of bed which is where he stayed for the rest of the week. He blamed it all on a cold, but I knew the real reason. By the weekend, he seemed fine again.

I made the decision to give my notice in at work. I wasn't coping and although the visits from my mum had subsided, they still concerned me.

Could I be losing my grip? Or maybe I was having a temporary blip to help me get through these tough times.

I missed Mum not being around, weird as it seemed. She'd been a fantastic help over the past week or so, although, in my rational mind, I knew this couldn't be possible.

As a child, I remembered Mum and Dad having terrible fights. Mum would smash furniture, pots and pans, ornaments, mirrors, in fact, anything that got in her way. Dad put up with more than most men would. However, Mum's crazy behaviour would make him flip his lid and he'd lash out at her, if only to stop her hurting one of us.

Mum used to scream the place down and the neighbours would call the police. Instead of taking Dad away, the police knew Mum was the real abuser. In fact, on occasion, she even attacked the police as they entered the property.

My first happy interlude was when I was eight years old. Mum had been marched off by the police and was gone for weeks. Dad and I settled into a normal and easy routine. I would go to school, he would go to work and we would cook dinner together and play games in the evenings. He taught me how to play chess and we had some terrific tournaments. Of course, Dad always won but I gave a good game.

One day, I came home from school and she met me at the front gate.

Things seemed fine at first. Mum took over the household chores and even cooked proper meals for us when we returned home in the evening. Dad and I began to relax and stopped tiptoeing around her.

Until she blew up again, that is.

There were no warning signs, just sudden out and out destruction and mayhem. Then there was the mental and physical abuse.

This became a regular pattern for years, until one day, she never returned.

Dad blamed her for my condition. He tried his best to give me a stable and secure home life after that, but the damage had already been done. At twelve years old I first attempted suicide and was diagnosed with bipolar disorder.

I never saw Mum again. Dad said she'd completely left the building—gone nutty he meant.

She died when I was nineteen years old. Dad and I were the only ones at her funeral.

After her death, my problems seemed to settle down. I began to sleep in my bed, instead of underneath. I got a job at the local post office sorting mail. By the time I met Gavin I was pretty much normal.

Or so I thought.

My specialist insisted I stayed on the meds, and apart from a few wobbly moments after giving birth to each of the children, I'd had no real problems. However, it seemed as soon as my idyllic life hit a bump in the road, the odd behaviour returned and with a vengeance.

Since Gavin had been sick and holed up in his room, I'd once again taken control and assumed the role of nursemaid. My life seemed to function much better with a purpose. I'd lost that purpose for a while there, but I now felt back on track.

Gavin was my husband and I was his wife, in sickness and in health.

So I slotted back into my daily routine and by Sunday it was as though the past month hadn't even happened.

Chapter 15

Adam didn't know how a full week passed by so fast, but he was glad it had.

He'd arranged to take Amanda to the movies tonight and for a bite of supper afterwards. After listing all the new release movies, Amanda made a suggestion of her own.

He suspected she intended to test his romantic tolerance levels when she chose the classic showing of Wuthering Heights.

Adam had heard of it. Who hadn't? Kate Bush had even sung about it, but other than that, he knew nothing.

Amanda, dressed more casually than she had last week, looked stunning in her brown slacks, red jersey and black high heeled boots.

She didn't invite him in this time, stepping through the front door as he pulled up outside.

Amanda ordered a huge box of popcorn and a chocolate topped ice-cream to take into the theatre. He considered suggesting they share her popcorn but thought she might think him a cheapskate, so he decided to order a small one for himself instead.

The movie wasn't all gushy and romantic and beautiful as he'd imagined. The powerful and raw emotions in the first few scenes amazed him, and he felt gutted when Heathcliff went away.

Amanda sniffled and he turned to see her crying into her popcorn. As the tears poured down her cheeks, she looked up and smiled at him.

Whether it was the melancholy feelings the movie had provoked in him, or the heart-wrenching, thought-provoking situation the characters found themselves in, or even the old English romantic way the actors spoke, but she caused his heart to miss a beat. He knew he loved her at that very moment.

By the end of the movie, he was beside himself. He'd been certain there would be a *happy-ever-after* ending.

As the main character, Cathy, died, a sob caught in his throat and he could barely breathe. A knot in his stomach seemed to be curling in on itself and he feared a physical injury might be occurring. He brushed away a couple of tears and coughed.

He left the cinema with a heavy heart. He never imagined these feelings could be caused by a movie.

Still sobbing by the time they got to the car, Amanda said, "That was lovely." She wiped her eyes on a scrap of tissue. "Poor Heathcliff."

"Lovely?" he cried, horrified. "You've got to be joking. I thought old movies were all sweetness and light. I've never been so distraught in all my life!" He stared at her, shaking his head.

Amanda burst out laughing and a snot bubble blew from her nose. There was a brief pause as they stared at each other, unsure of what to say—then they burst out laughing.

Adam couldn't regain control of himself and they were both reduced to hysterical wrecks.

"Never would have thought—" Amanda snorted. "—that we would be laughing after ..." Amanda held her stomach before continuing. "... such a beautiful film," she said in a high-pitched voice.

Adam couldn't reply. He couldn't breathe. He couldn't remember the last time he'd laughed so hard.

This woman was good for him.

Afterwards, they went for pizza. They were so easy together, and Adam found himself opening up about his past, telling her more than he'd told anybody before.

"I never thought about your situation when I suggested the film. How insensitive of me," she said.

"To be honest, I didn't associate any of it with Sarah. She never suffered in front of me, her death was over and done with in a flash, leaving an empty hole where my heart had been." He smiled and rubbed his stubbly jaw. "Not very macho I know."

Amanda reached for his hand across the table. Her eyes full of compassion and understanding, but not pity. He hated pity.

"I sometimes think, although illness is terrible, and watching a person you love waste away before your very eyes must be the worst thing ever." He shrugged. "But at least you get to prepare for it—to plan what you'll do with your life—albeit tentatively. With a sudden death, it feels as though you've been hit by a juggernaut, but your mind is paralysed instead of your body."

"I know that feeling," Amanda said. "Things happening all around you as though you're in some kind of a bubble."

"Exactly." Adam nodded.

"Don't you struggle having to deal with death and deliver devastating news day in day out the way you do?"

"Yeah, of course, but I can't stop these things from happening by refusing to do my job. I can, however, help those left behind by trying to make sense of what has happened to their loved ones and by bringing the culprit to justice."

"It must be hard on you when you can't solve a crime, or when you do, but don't get the satisfaction of getting the person to pay for their crimes."

They both knew they were talking, once again, about her brother. Andrew had escaped after killing three of the paedophiles that had abused them both repeatedly as children—one of them being their own father.

"There are certain situations when even I want the bad guys to get away. Obviously, I would arrest them and go through the motions if the opportunity present- ed itself—I'm a detective first and foremost. But in your brother's case, what he did by ridding the world of those disgusting creatures—I kind of applaud him."

Amanda's eyes filled with tears and she bent her head, wiping them away with her napkin.

"Not that I'd admit what I just said to anyone else, of course. My job would be on the line, you understand?"

She nodded and smiled, squeezing his hand. "Per- fectly."

Chapter 16

The week progressed smoothly. My mother, apart from the odd little snippet of interference, had been rather quiet.

By Wednesday, I felt good and much more settled.

I decided to call the girls for a catch up, the first in a while.

The phone answered on the first ring and I was deafened by Stella screaming in my ear.

"Hang on a minute, I'm pulling over."

I shook my head—my youngest daughter never failed to irritate me.

"Hello, Mum. Sorry about that—I'm just on my way home from work?"

"Hi Stella, are you all right to chat or should I call back later?"

"No, you're fine. I intended to ring you when I got home anyway. Guess what?"

"I give in, tell me," I said, too exhausted to play guessing games.

"I've been promoted," she squealed.

"Fantastic news. Still doing the same thing?" Stella lived in France with her partner Tina and they both worked in the wastewater industry. Not a job for a young woman in my opinion, but she seemed to enjoy it.

"Kinda, I'm going to have to study again, but I don't mind that."

"I'm pleased for you, love. How's Tina?"

"She's good. Claudie's not well though. Tina stayed home with him today."

"She took a day off work for a dog?" My lip curled, and my voice gave away my thoughts on the subject. They treated Claude, their giant poodle, like a baby.

"He's not *just* a dog, Mother. He's *our* dog."

Soon after, I hung up and gave Yvonne a quick ring.

She told me her and Keith planned to try for a baby after Krystal's wedding.

This news had been all I'd dreamed of since they got married four years ago. I'd begun to think they'd never be ready to start a family, but now it might actually happen. Yet, instead of the euphoria I'd expected, I felt emotionally flat. For Vonny's sake, I tried to I tried to sound excited.

Since deciding to give up work, I'd been much better. Not that I had a stressful job. The added pressure on top of everything had almost pushed me over the edge and I had no intention of getting to that point again.

On Thursday morning, Gavin told me he would be staying away for the night and everything came crashing down around me.

I don't know why you're so surprised. Did you think just because a couple of his boyfriends bit the dust he would stop?

I ignored her. Tried to shut her out and continue as normal but by lunchtime we were having full-on conversations again.

Have you checked where he is?

"Ten minutes ago he was at the office."

And now?

"For God's sake!" I snatched my mobile off the table and glanced at the screen. "Still at the office," I snapped.

Are you sorted and ready to go once he's on the move?

"I don't think I'm going anywhere this time."

I knew it! I bloody knew it.

"You know nothing, Mother. Keep your nose out."

Charming, here I am trying to be of help and you speak to me like that.

"I'm not speaking to you like anything. You're not even here you've been dead thirty-odd years."

Do I sound dead, to you?

My nerves were close to frazzled. The familiar cloud seemed to be settling around me and I was scared of what it meant.

And then I wasn't.

Good girl.

Once again, I dressed in Gavin's clothing and re-trieved the pillowcase from the airing cupboard. Sitting at the dining table, I waited for my husband to make a move.

At just before 2pm he left the office and headed for the motorway.

As I was about to leave, I had an idea. I walked back to the kitchen, rummaged about in the junk draw-er and found what I was looking for. Placing the key in my bra, I headed out the door.

Moments later I hit the motorway heading for Lon-don.

***

Anthony Kingsley got out of his top-of-the-range metallic grey Honda and flashed his hazel eyes up and down the road. With no other cars in sight he growled, raked his fingers through his close-cropped dark blond hair and kicked the tyre.

"Bloody heap of shit!" he muttered through gritted teeth. He glanced at his watch. Three o'clock already.

He should be on the other side of town by now. He'd never make the meeting on time.

Back behind the wheel, he cursed the car once again. His last car hadn't come with all the fancy gadgets and gizmos this one had, but ran on the sniff of an oily rag without any problems at all.

This one had been in the shop three times already, and he'd not even had it six months yet. To top it all off, he'd allowed his RAC subscription to lapse.

"Fuck!" He slammed his hand on the steering wheel. Clearing his throat, he reached for his mobile, and after trawling through his numbers, he dialled.

"Gavin May."

"Hi, Mr May, Tony Kingsley here. I'm supposed to be meeting with you today—twenty minutes from now, in fact," he said.

"Yes, of course, Tony. What can I do for you?"

"My car broke down. I'm running late."

"I tell you what. I haven't got any other appointments booked, so how about you give me a call once you're sorted, presuming you still want to meet up?"

"Definitely. I appreciate your understanding. Thanks, Mr May."

With a sigh, Tony hung up and dialled another number.

"Dave, Tony here. Any chance you can sort out this piece of shit car? I need to get into town asap for a meeting."

"Sorry, Tone, no can do. I'm flat stick and on my own today. Best I can do for you is tow the car in once

I finish up for the day. Text me the location and leave the keys on top of the front tyre."

Oh, this day was going from bad to worse. A superstitious man might take this as a sign that he shouldn't go ahead with the business deal after all. He dialled his wife, his last hope.

"Susan, you'll never guess. My car's gone and bloody died again. I'm stuck on Harbet Road. Where are you?"

"Oh heck, I'm still at the orthopaedic specialists. Cheryl's just had her X-ray and we're waiting for the doctor to take a look. I'm going to have to wait. We've been stuck here all afternoon."

"Of course, any idea how long you might be?"

"Can't you phone your Phil?" Her voice sounded irritable.

"I can't. Remember, he's gone to that convention with Sam today."

"Oh yeah, I forgot. Okay, you'll have to wait for me. I'll get to you as soon as I can."

An hour later, his wife parked her car behind his. He rang Gavin back.

"Hi it's Tony again. I have a ride. Where would you like to meet?"

"Come straight to my motel if you like. There's a bar in the restaurant which is good a place as any."

Tony jotted down the address and hung up. He locked the car and put the keys on top of the tyre.

He bundled his briefcase and jacket into the foot-well as he climbed into the passenger seat of his wife's red Mitsubishi. His eighteen-month-old twins, Damien and Cheryl squealed with delight when they saw him.

"Hello, my babies." He kissed Susan on the cheek before handing her the address.

"I know where that is," she said, manoeuvring the car into the road.

"How did you get on with the specialist?" Tony asked.

"Fine. They think she'll grow out of it, but will send for us in a few months to make sure."

Cheryl's left foot had started turning in as she walked. It didn't seem to bother her, but the doctor had been worried in case there was some underlying prob-lem.

"That's good news, then."

"How will you get home?" Susan said as she parked outside the motel.

"I'll get a taxi—shouldn't be more than a tenner from here." Anthony got out of the car and walked round to the driver's side.

Susan wound her window down and he bent to kiss her.

"Thanks, Suze. I owe you big time."

"You sure do," she laughed. "Don't forget the twins. They'll go berserk if you take off without making a fuss of them."

"I would never forget my two favourite little people." He jumped in the back, causing a commotion of hysterical belly-laughs as he kissed and tickled Damian and Cheryl. He climbed back out and waved at them as Susan drove away.

Standing his briefcase between his feet, he shrugged into his jacket, before walking into the bar.

Gavin waved as he entered.

Tony made a drinking motion, pointing at the bar, but Gavin shook his head. He ordered himself a rum and coke before joining Gavin.

They'd met in person once before, at an insurance seminar Gavin had held, and they'd been corresponding ever since. Tony had been an insurance broker in his own one-man team for the past thirteen years. He had gone to a seminar to see what all the fuss was about and had been impressed with what Gavin's company offered.

Tony would be able to afford the initial investment, at a push, using Susan's inheritance. If Gavin's figures were correct, with his company's backing, Tony would be raking it in by the end of next year. His dream was to employ a team of people and expand the business outside the London area.

They exchanged small talk for the first ten minutes or so, before getting down to the business at hand.

"So, from what I can gather, you're thinking about going ahead with our proposal?" Gavin asked.

Tony nodded. "I am, yes."

"What took so long? I'll be honest with you, I've been in negotiations with other businesses in your area, but as yet nothing has been signed."

"I was nervous at first—it's a big step. I've built up a decent name for myself over the years and worked my arse off to put it bluntly. Recently I've been struggling to compete with the big boys. My hands are tied since the changes to the industry. I find I'm losing business hand over fist."

Gavin nodded. "I see, and yes this is a huge step for you, I appreciate that. However, I can honestly say that, with our help, you will *be* one of the big boys yourself soon enough."

"That's what I need, and with all the other services I'll be able to offer, I'll be unstoppable."

"Sounds like a done deal then," Gavin said. "Did you bring the paperwork I sent you?"

"I did, I have them right here." Tony opened his briefcase, pulled out a manila folder and handed it to Gavin.

Gavin flicked through the stack of papers. "I can't seem to find the signature page of the contract."

Tony bounced the palm of his hand on his forehead. "I'm so sorry. I must have left it at home. I can send a courier parcel to you in the morning."

"No problem, there's a copy in my room. If you don't mind, we can quickly grab it before you leave?"

"Yeah, great. Now if that concludes our meeting I suggest another drink—my shout, and how about a bite to eat?"

"Don't mind if I do." Gavin smiled.

Chapter 17

By the time I arrived in Pinevale, Gavin was already at the motel.

I parked behind several huge trucks in the freight company's car park next door to the motel and waited. I had a perfect view of the units and the motel car park through the chain-link fence and bushes.

Over an hour later, Gavin emerged from his room and headed into the restaurant at the front of the building. I got out of the car and stood close to the fence, watching closely in case he came back out.

When a car pulled up on the other side of the fence right beside me, I could hear the conversation of the couple within. The guy got out and walked round the car and kissed the female driver.

"Thanks, Suze, I owe you big time," he said.

"You sure do," she said, good-naturedly. "Don't for-get the twins. They'll go berserk if you take off without making a fuss of them."

"I would never forget my two favourite little people."

I chuckled to myself as he opened the back doors and clambered inside, making a huge display of kiss-ing the two squealing kiddies.

The car drove off and the man entered the restau-rant.

I desperately needed to find a toilet. I pressed my hand to the top of my legs and clenched, worried I might pee my pants.

You have your phone. If he goes anywhere, you'll know.

"Ah, yes," I whispered. I'd forgotten about that.

In the restaurant across the road, I ordered a take-away coffee and used the bathroom.

Gavin still hadn't moved when I returned. I climbed back into the car to wait.

A while later Gavin appeared at the restaurant door. I got out of the car, trying to see who he held the door open for.

My stomach flipped as I realised Gavin's companion was the man with the twins.

I shook my head. No matter how much I seemed to prepare myself, this situation never failed to disgust me.

Thinking about the delicious little twins I'd seen him fussing over earlier, an immense anger once again exploded within me.

Stay calm. You know what you need to do.

Oh, I knew all right. I needed to stop this once and for all.

Once they were inside the unit, I reached inside my car, grabbed the cap from the passenger seat and pulled it snugly onto my head. Then I grabbed the wrench wrapped in the pillowcase.

Once again, I kept to the fence-line and ran in short bursts, stopping to hide and look around a couple of times when possible.

There were three cars parked up. The middle one was Gavin's. As I reached it, I fumbled inside my bra and pulled out the key I'd taken from the house earlier. I hit the centre button and the side lights flashed and I heard the doors unlock.

Climbing inside, the interior lights stayed illuminated for the longest minute of my life. I was beside myself, certain Gavin would come out and catch me red handed. But he didn't.

I slid down in the driver's seat and lay in wait.

After around twenty minutes, a cab pulled up outside the unit and tooted its horn.

Gavin opened the door and waved to the driver and then shook hands with his friend. He watched until the cab backed out of the car park before going back inside, closing the door behind him.

I needed to act fast. I clocked the direction the cab headed, started up Gavin's car and caught up—keeping just enough distance between us not to draw attention to myself.

***

After a couple more drinks and a bar meal, Tony and Gavin strolled to Gavin's motel unit where they both signed the all-important contract.

"So, I guess that's it," Tony said.

"Yes, for now. I'm not sure when things will happen, but I'll get the Branding team to keep you in the loop. Welcome aboard."

Gavin held his hand towards him and Tony shook it enthusiastically.

"Can I call a cab?"

"Of course, feel free." Gavin indicated the phone at the side of the bed.

The taxi arrived ten minutes later and Tony said his goodbyes.

He had a great feeling about this. Susan had been worried, but he'd managed to convince her it was the right thing to do.

Granted, all their savings would be used up and more besides, but if what Gavin said was true, they'd replace every penny in no time.

He got the taxi driver to drop him off on the main road at the top of his street. The twins had always been light sleepers and he thought the taxi's noisy diesel engine would wake them.

Tony paid the driver and gave him a generous tip, then turned towards home.

The navy blue car came from nowhere. It mounted the curb and rammed him into the brick wall beside him.

A million thoughts raced through his mind at once. One of them being how lucky the car had missed the briefcase he held at shoulder height, in front of him. He realised how stupid this was, considering the car had pinned him to the wall. He didn't feel any pain though—tremendous shock and confusion, but thankfully no pain.

His surprise and shock were mirrored in the wide-eyed stare of the driver. Her gaunt grey face seemed close enough for him to reach out and touch.

She reversed the car and stopped.

Tony expected her to get out, to come racing to his aid, begging his forgiveness. He could hear screams and a voice yelling for someone to call an ambulance. Everything seemed to be happening in slow motion and he winced as his hand touched the ground, realising he'd slid down the wall.

He lifted his head and saw the car hurtling towards him again.

Chapter 18

Mum had taken over by the time we'd caught up with the taxi. I was merely a spectator.

I thought she'd do what we'd planned the last time, but I couldn't have been more wrong.

We slowed the car as the twins' dad got out of the cab, and we watched as he turned into a side street. I presumed we would pass him and park the car further up the street. However, Mum had other ideas.

As the car struck him I screamed, and my head collided with the steering wheel. It had taken a couple of seconds before I realised what had happened. Until I saw the man hunched over the bonnet of the car, staring straight at me. His right hand held his briefcase up and out at a strange angle.

We shot backwards and the sound of tearing metal filled my ears. I expected Mum to speed away, but instead, in true horror film fashion, she darted forward once again.

I managed to brace myself to avoid another bang on the head.

The street began filling up with people and their screams were deafening.

The car backed up once more, before speeding off towards the motel. Something metallic sounding scraped along the road as we drove, making an ear-splitting noise that would set anybody's teeth on edge.

Tears streamed down my face.

Pull yourself together. Do you want to get us caught?

Unable to speak, I shook my head frantically.

Mum drove to the motel car park. I expected the grating noise the car made to bring everyone out of their units, but it didn't.

She stuffed the pillowcase underneath the passenger seat and placed the cap in the glove box.

We climbed from the steaming, hissing vehicle, taking care to lock the doors.

Wasting no time, we ran to my car, and soon sped off in the direction of the motorway.

Half way home I realised I was back in control.

I replayed what had happened in my mind and touched the bump on my forehead as I remembered the first collision.

Gavin would be done for, now. With all the evidence against him, he wouldn't be able to hurt another family *ever* again.

I shuddered.

What Mum had done was for the best. However, now Gavin's secret would be known to the world, including Yvonne and Stella. But what choice had there been? I couldn't protect myself and my girls at the expense of all the other sweet and innocent people. No, this was the only way short of killing him.

Pulling off the motorway, I stopped at the first layby bordering a copse of trees and I threw Gavin's key into the thick of them.

My phone showed Gavin still at the motel, but I didn't think it would be too long before they found him.

I pulled up in front of the house, relieved nobody seemed to be around to notice me arrive home at 10pm.

Once inside, I called Gavin's phone, conscious I would need keep my voice as steady as possible. I didn't care if he answered or not. A message would be as effective, but he answered.

"Hello, sweetheart, I've been meaning to call you, but was just finalising some paperwork."

"That's nice." My tone sounded flat. "I've got a headache and was just off to bed, thought I'd say goodnight."

"Oh dear. Yeah, you get an early night. You'll feel better in the morning. Did you take any aspirin?"

"I'll get a couple now and get my head down. Good-night, Gavin." I gripped the phone to my ear as he said goodnight and hung up.

I stripped off Gavin's sweats and threw them into the washer on a quick wash, then cleaned my shoes. Curling up on the sofa, I waited.

***

Adam lay with one leg balanced on the back of the sofa, holding his phone to his ear, a cheesy grin plastered on his face.

"So what do you want to do on Saturday?" he asked.

"Anything. Although I don't think you could cope with another classic movie, do you?" Amanda laughed.

"No! Definitely not. I think I'll be traumatized by the last one for weeks." He laughed too.

"Oh well, you choose, I'm easy. You know the kids will be here this weekend so you won't be able to come back this time."

"I gathered that. Shame though. I had a great time last week."

"Me too, but we can anticipate next week," she said in a sexy, breathy voice.

"I suggest you don't purr at me like that if you want me to be patient. Otherwise, I'll be over there in a flash, a-tap-tap-tapping on your window," he groaned.

She squealed. "No, you can't do that. I'll behave, I promise."

They'd had such a nice evening on Saturday. The last thing he'd expected to do was take their relationship further, but it seemed the most natural thing to do.

His phone began buzzing in his ear.

"I've gotta go, Mand, another call is coming in. Have a think about Saturday and I'll call you tomorrow night."

The phone began ringing as soon as he hung up.

"Stanley."

"It's me," Frances said. "There's been a homicide in Pinevale West. Anthony Kingsley, 38. Hit by a car, twice. Witnesses say it was no accident."

"I'll be right there. Send the address."

Adam leapt from the sofa and into the bedroom, donning the clothes he'd got out of not half an hour ago.

The victim was a broken mess.

The first collision had shattered his bottom half—the second killed him outright, crushing his upper body and his head.

One of the witnesses had seen him before the second impact and recognised him. The contents of the briefcase confirmed his identity.

He found Susan Kingsley pacing in the lounge of their large terraced house.

Adam introduced both himself and Frances and indicated she take a seat.

"I can't sit down. Somebody needs to arrest Steven. Has anybody even gone over there yet?" she said, her voice irate.

Relieved she wasn't a blubbering mess, Adam needed to take advantage before the tears set in.

"Calm down, Mrs Kingsley. I haven't a clue what you're talking about."

"I already told the officer. Tony's brother, Steven. He's been bugging us for weeks now, wanting us to invest in some crazy business scheme or other. He knew I'd got an inheritance from my Gran and he wanted to get his greedy mitts on it."

"Why do you think he would have gone to these extremes?" Adam asked.

"Because Tony phoned him this morning and told him that he had no intention investing, that he'd chosen to use the money to expand our own business instead. Steven was angry. I could hear the abuse he dished out from the other side of the room."

Adam nodded, glancing at Frances who raised her eyebrows.

Susan continued. "It has to be him—the neighbour said she saw a blue car and Steven owns a blue car."

"Okay, we'll get someone to check him out, I promise you. In the meantime, we need some more details. Can I get one of the officers to make you a cup of tea?" Adam said.

She shook her head and sat on the edge of the sofa.

"Could you tell me where your husband has been tonight, Mrs Kingsley?"

"I dropped him off for a business meeting at a motel. The address is on a slip of paper in my car," she said.

Adam nodded at the uniformed officer standing in the doorway. The officer nodded back and left.

"Did you often take him to his appointments?" Frances asked.

"His car broke down earlier. He said he'd get a taxi home as the motel wasn't far from here."

"Your husband has his own business, is that correct?" Adam said.

"Yes. He's an insurance broker."

"Do you know if he has any enemies?"

"No. Just his dodgy brother. Who else would want to hurt my poor Tony?" She began to wail.

Adam found it astonishing the amount of ways there were to cry. He'd seen them all hundreds of times over. Most people, even in the deepest throes of grief, will cover their mouths and try to have a little self-respect. But some, including Susan Kingsley, just cry freely. Letting their mouths hang open.

This type of grief embarrassed Adam. He clasped his hands and glanced at Frances, who was busy scribbling everything in her notebook.

After a couple of minutes, he said. "Mrs Kingsley. I know you've had a terrible shock, but please, I need you to focus if we have any chance of catching the person responsible."

She wiped her eyes and cleared her throat, and a triple hiccup escaped her.

"Thank you. Now, we will need a list of your husband's clients. Especially those who had made a recent claim," he said.

"It's all at the office. I can get it for you, but the twins are in bed."

"Tomorrow will do. Now is there anybody who can come to stay with you?"

"Tony's other brother, Phil. Oh my God, I need to tell Phil." Another bout of sobs followed.

The officer returned and handed Adam a piece of paper as he got to his feet. It had a name and address of the motel, he handed it to Frances.

"Just one last thing, Mrs Kingsley. Do you know the name of the man your husband met at the motel?"

"Yes, Gavin. Gavin May."

"Thanks. If you give Officer Newly your brother-in-law's number, I'm sure he'll be happy to call him for you."

Adam nodded to Frances and they headed out of the door.

"Have you interviewed the witnesses?" he asked as they stepped out onto the street.

"Yes. I have all their statements. None of them saw the first crash, the noise brought them all running. However, they all said the same thing—the car reversed and a couple of seconds later, as the victim slid to the ground, it slammed forward and finished the job."

"Did anybody see the driver?"

"Just that they wore a dark cap with gold lettering."

"Number plate? Car details?"

"A partial number plate, LM60 something, something, D. It was a navy blue, Toyota Camry. I've radioed the details through," Frances said.

"Fancy accompanying me to see what Steven Kingsley has to say?"

"Try stopping me." She smiled.

The address wasn't too far away and nothing like Adam had imagined from Mrs Kingsley's description of the snivelling, money grabbing brother.

The detached house sat on a nice sized plot on a tree-lined street. Adam whistled as they parked his Mondeo on the road.

The property was in darkness.

They climbed the steps and Adam rang the doorbell.

Moments later a light came on upstairs followed by a series of bumps and somebody muttering to themselves behind the door as they hooked the chain in place.

The door opened and a man in his forties peeked through the small gap.

"Steven Kingsley?" Adam asked.

The man nodded, his eyebrows screwed together.

Adam flashed his badge and Frances did the same.

"DI Adam Stanley and DS Holly Frances," Adam said. "Can we have a word with you, sir?"

"What the hell for at this time of night?"

"If we could just come in first, sir."

The door closed and Mr Kingsley removed the chain, before opening the door fully.

Steven Kingsley wore a t-shirt and shorts. He ushered them into the first room on the right, off the impressive hallway, and switched on the main light.

Quality furnishings adorned the immaculately presented, room. Greys, blacks and whites were broken up with the odd splash of burnt orange. It reminded Adam of something out of home and garden magazine.

"Now what can I do for you, Detectives?" Steven asked.

"We need to know your whereabouts at eight-thirty this evening, sir?" Adam said.

"Here. Why?"

"Do you have any witnesses to that?"

"Yes, my wife and daughter. What's this all about?"

"There was a hit and run this evening, sir. You have been named as a possible suspect."

"Me? Is this some kind of a joke?"

"I can assure you, it's no joke, sir," Adam said.

"Who was it? I assume I must know them," Steven said.

"Your brother—Anthony Kingsley."

Steven gasped and shuffled back a couple of steps on unsteady feet, his hand flew to his throat. "Tony? Our Tony? Is he okay?"

"I'm afraid not, sir. Mr Kingsley died at the scene."

Steven Kingsley woke his wife, Carina, a woman at least fifteen years his junior. After a brief conversation with her and an inspection of their blue Mercedes, Adam and Frances left the house.

"What a waste of time that was. Now what?" he asked.

Frances flicked through her notes. We're just about to pass the motel if you want to check it out?"

Adam nodded. "Why not."

Soon after, they pulled into the motel carpark and Adam got out, heading for the reception.

A buzzer sounded as he stepped inside and a flustered looking bald man in his late fifties stumbled out of the door behind the desk.

"The sign says no vacancies," he snapped.

"We're not after a room, sir," Adam said, flashing his badge. "Could you tell me which room Gavin May is in."

The guy checked the diary. "Unit three. Is everything all right?"

"Perfectly, thank you. Goodnight, sir."

As Adam walked outside and noticed the expression on Frances' face. He turned to see what she was staring at.

A navy blue Camry had been parked up at an angle with the front smashed in. On closer inspection, he could see blood and tissue in the grooves of the grill.

Adam called the station for backup and within minutes the carpark was filled with flashing blue lights.

Adam tapped on the door of unit three.

Nothing.

He tried once more, louder this time, and he heard movement inside.

"One minute," a man's voice called out.

The door was opened by a middle-aged man dressed in boxer shorts and a white vest. He squinted and blinked at Adam and Frances, and then at the mass of uniforms outside.

"Mr May?"

He nodded.

"Mr Gavin May?"

"Yes, what is it?"

We'll need you to accompany us to the station, sir. Can you get your trousers on, please?"

Adam pushed his way past Gavin and checked the room. Once satisfied Mr May wasn't a danger to them he waved to the uniformed officers.

"I don't understand. What is this all about?"

"Mr May, I am arresting you for the murder of Anthony Kingsley. You do not have to say anything, but it may harm your defence if you do not mention when questioned, something which you later rely on in court. Anything you do say may be given in evidence."

Chapter 19

"What the hell?" Gavin boomed. Stepping back and throwing his arms up to stop Frances from placing the handcuffs on his wrist.

"I suggest you calm down, sir," Adam said, taking the handcuffs from Frances and squaring up to Gavin, who was at least a head shorter.

"But, I haven't done anything. Tony left here in one piece--you can check with the cab office. I haven't left the room since."

"Then you have nothing to worry about, sir. Please co-operate." Adam picked up the grey trousers from the chair next to the bed and shoved them towards Gavin. "Get them on."

Gavin snatched the trousers and thrust each foot into them with exaggerated and erratic movements.

"This is an injustice. I'm a respectable business man. Why the hell would I hurt anyone? Especially the client I've just signed up after months of trying."

He grabbed his jacket off the back of the chair and put it on over his vest, before stamping into his shoes.

"Turn 'round, please, sir." Adam held up the handcuffs.

"There's no need for that, detective. I'm not going to be a problem."

"Not an option, I'm afraid," Adam said as he placed one cuff on Gavin's right wrist.

"For fuck's sake." Gavin turned and allowed Adam to cuff his left. "What about my stuff?"

"It can stay here 'till later," Adam said.

"Get away from there," Gavin yelled at the crowd of officers around his car as they left the unit. The words seemed to stick in his throat as he clocked the damaged vehicle.

"Who's done that to my car?" he said. His eyes were wide, the colour drained from his face as he shook his head.

Adam opened his car door. "Get in please, sir."

Once Gavin was in the car, Adam turned to Frances and raised his eyebrows.

"Good acting?" she said.

"Who knows? Bloody convincing though," Adam said.

He stepped back into the unit and glanced around. He saw nothing out of the ordinary, a shirt on the back of a chair, a briefcase on the table, a few clothes hung in the wardrobe and an empty sports bag on the wardrobe floor. He picked up a bunch of car keys from the kitchen bench. This wasn't a crime scene. The car, however, was a different story.

He left the unit, closing the door behind him.

Adam and Frances stood outside the interview room watching Gavin pace the floor through the two-way mirror.

As they were about to enter, a uniformed officer rushed into the corridor.

"You may want to see this, sir," he said, passing Adam a pink pillowcase.

Adam took it from him and glanced inside. He felt his stomach drop to his boots as the realisation dawned.

"What?" Frances took the pillowcase. Her mouth gaped open. "Are you kidding me?"

Adam shook his head in disbelief. "Arrange a DNA test of Mr May and get this to forensics," he said to the uniformed officer.

"Yes, sir."

"You ready for this?" Adam turned back to Frances.

She nodded, clearly still distracted.

"Let's do it." He strode ahead of her into the room.

"About time," Gavin said. "Will somebody tell me what's happening?"

"All in good time, Mr May," Frances said as she prepared the recording device for the interview.

"Take a seat," Adam said.

Gavin sat down on the vinyl covered seat. He scraped the metal chair legs across the floor making a loud noise.

Adam sat next to Frances.

Frances organised the tape recorder and stated their names before sitting next to Adam.

"Okay, Mr May. Can we begin with the events of last night?" Adam said.

"I told you. I met Tony Kingsley in the bar at the motel. He'd had a problem with his car and so we changed the location to suit him. After the meeting, we had a bite to eat and a couple of drinks."

"And then what?" Adam said.

"We went to my unit to sign the contract. Mr Kingsley rang for a taxi and left. End of."

"What time was that?" Frances asked.

"I'm not sure. Eight—half past—somewhere around there."

"What did you do afterwards?" Adam said.

"I still had paperwork to do regarding Tony's—sorry Mr Kingsley's business deal. That's how I spent the rest of the evening."

"Did you see or speak to anybody after that?"

"Just my wife. She called before she went to bed."

"What time?"

"I'm not sure. It must have been—" he shrugged, "—tennish."

Adam cleared his throat. "Do you know a man called Carl Pilkington?"

Gavin sucked in air too quickly and began to choke.

Adam glanced at Frances and they both raised their eyebrows at each other.

"So, Mr May. Can you answer the question, please?" Adam asked again once Gavin had stopped coughing.

"Yes. I didn't know his name though until I saw him on the news."

"But you knew him?"

Gavin nodded.

"Please Mr May, for the benefit of the tape," Frances said.

"Yes. I met him the night he died," Gavin said.

"What for?" Adam said.

"Sorry?"

"I said, what reason did you meet him and where?" Adam said.

Gavin shook his head and shrugged.

"It may help you to be honest with us if I tell you we're aware Mr Pilkington had had sexual intercourse before he died and will be able to match his partner with DNA results."

Gavin, his face now turned a pallid white, shrugged again.

"For the tape, Mr May is shrugging his shoulders," Frances said.

"Mr May?" Adam pressed.

"Yeah, all right. We met for sex, that doesn't mean I killed him though."

Adam took a deep breath and sat back in his chair, stretching. Then he scratched his head.

"I know what it looks like—but honestly—it's got nothing to do with me," Gavin insisted.

"How about Joseph Bates?"

Gavin closed his eyes and sighed, sweat beading on his top lip.

"Mr May?" Gavin said again.

"I met him last week."

"When?"

"The night he died."

"You do see why we might be having a problem believing you're innocent in all of this—don't you?" Adam asked.

Gavin nodded. "I know how it looks. I've been going over it since last week. In fact, I did consider contacting you myself but I knew I'd be in the frame. I'm not stupid."

"Maybe you could explain to us then, how the murder weapon made it under the passenger seat of your car—the car used to murder Anthony Kingsley last night."

"I don't know—it's not mine. I need to call my solicitor. Someone is fitting me up."

"As you wish, sir."

***

I hadn't expected to, but I eventually fell asleep sitting up.

Waking with a start, I checked my phone at just after 6am and discovered Gavin, to my horror, was still at the motel.

The plan hadn't worked after all.

My mind raced. I couldn't understand why. Heaps of witnesses saw which direction I'd headed and more than likely, a trail of car parts led all the way to the motel.

The twins' mum knew where he'd been. Not to mention, the state of the car itself.

I turned on the TV hoping for some news. But, as had been happening more and more of late, the noise that accompanied the program almost deafened me. I had no choice but to switch it off.

I needed a coffee, yet couldn't force myself up from the seated position I'd been in all night.

The garden gate clanged, followed by a hammering on the front door.

Dazed, I dragged myself to my feet and into the hall, trying to make out the shapes through the frosted glass panels.

Opening the door, I froze. The front garden and the street were filled with police officers. I figured they must have worked the truth out after all and had come to arrest me.

Keep calm—you know nothing!

I sighed with relief, Mum had returned. I didn't think I could face this alone.

"Mrs May?" a lady police officer said, her auburn hair pulled severely into a bun.

I nodded, unable to speak.

"My name is PC Morehouse. I have a warrant to search these premises." She held up a sheet of paper that I had no intention of reading.

Stunned, I took a step backwards and opened the door wide. A steady stream of people entered, some in uniform some not.

PC Morehouse put her hand on my arm and led me through to the lounge.

"Please take a seat, Mrs May. We will get this over with as soon as possible."

"Wha ..." I shook my head. "I don't understand."

"Please take a seat," she repeated.

I staggered backwards, my hands feeling for the edge of the sofa and sat down with a bump.

Two officers were going through everything in the lounge, flicking through every book, magazine and drawer. One of them even inspected the tissue box.

"Please," I said. "Please, tell me why?"

"Your husband has been arrested, in connection with a serious crime."

"That's impossible. Are you sure? Gavin—Gavin May?"

"I'm afraid so, Mrs May."

Keep it up, Melissa. You're very convincing.

"What's he done?" I asked as she took a seat opposite me. She had, no doubt, been assigned to stay with me and keep me out of the way.

"I'm afraid I'm not at liberty to say. Somebody will inform you soon enough, I'm sure," she said in a soothing tone.

"Where is he?" I asked.

"At the station, being questioned." She offered me a weak smile. "Can I get you a hot drink or anything, Mrs May?"

I nodded. "Yes please. And I'll need to use the bathroom if that's all right."

"Certainly, give me one second." She left the room and when she returned, beckoned for me to follow her.

The bathroom was tidy, yet I could tell things had been moved. I straightened the pewter rose ornament on the windowsill a fraction to the left and shook my head. What they would be looking for underneath or inside that, I had no idea.

I felt a pang of intense anger at the intrusion. If this had come out of the blue, I would be hopping mad by now. However, I didn't have the energy nor the inclination to make a fuss, I just wanted all this over and done with.

As I came out of the bathroom, I bumped into a man carrying our computer hard-drive. He ducked past me and out the front door. Several bags filled with Gavin's clothing and shoes were piled in the hall.

"Where are they taking my computer?" I asked PC Morehouse.

"It will be examined and should be back to you in no time."

Once they left, I felt exhausted—mentally and physically.

Moments later, another knock sounded at the door. I groaned. I couldn't cope with any more right now.

My good friends and neighbours, Ken and Liz, stood on the doorstep.

Liz had always been bad with her nerves, but today she was shaking and wringing her hands as though on the verge of a panic attack. Her breath escaped in short gasps.

"Mel, what the heck is going on? Are you all right?" Ken grasped my hands.

I nodded and led them into the lounge.

"I don't know what's going on," I said, glancing at them both as I sat back down. "They said Gavin's been arrested for a serious crime."

Liz gasped.

"No! It must be some kind of mistake. Gavin's not a criminal," Ken said. "They took the computer, something's happened at work. Financial institutes are always under scrutiny. I bet you'll find this has nothing to do with him, Mel."

I nodded, liking this explanation and intending to use it myself. "Yeah, you're probably right."

They stayed long enough to make me another coffee and sandwich, which I couldn't eat. My stomach was queasy.

The police had done a thorough job. Nothing had been tipped up, but I could tell it wasn't right. Once alone again I busied myself, tidying up.

The GPS app still showed Gavin's phone at the motel.

I found today's paper on the kitchen worktop and quickly scanned it. Apart from a small article about a hit and run, no other details had been given.

I had no choice but to wait it out.

Chapter 20

The phone rang and I almost shot through the ceiling. I'd zoned out, for how long was anybody's guess.

"Hello," I said, my voice sounded croaky and I cleared my throat. "Hello," I said again.

"Is this Mrs Gavin May?" A well-spoken man asked.

"Yes."

"I'm calling from Mirage Motel in Pinevale."

My ears pricked up.

"Yes."

"Mrs May, this is a delicate matter, but are you aware your husband was arrested last night."

"Yes, I am," I said, confused why the motel would be contacting me.

"The thing is, your husband's belongings are still in the unit. We're fully booked at the moment and need to have permission to go in and pack them up. We will be able to store them for a short while if need be."

"What did the police say?" I asked.

"To contact you."

"Well, in that case, I'll come to collect them now."

"That's fine, there's no hurry so long as our cleaner can go into the unit to clean it. Would we be able to pack everything into his case? There isn't a lot."

"Yes, of course," I said, remembering I wasn't supposed to know where he was. "What's your address?"

After a quick wash and change of clothes, I left for London, worried somebody might recognise me or my car.

Mum had been quiet since last night, making a brief appearance when the police arrived this morning and nothing since. I could have done with her reassurance now.

The journey didn't seem to take as long for some reason. Gavin must have had a right old laugh at my expense all those years, staying away when he could easily have driven the ninety minutes home. Why had I never questioned it?

Arriving at the motel, I parked down the road a little way, not wanting to risk anyone recognising the car.

In the deserted reception, I rang the bell.

My stomach ached, as though I had half a dozen ping-pong balls belting around inside it.

A few moments later a red-faced man arrived, muttering to himself. He rolled his eyes when he noticed me.

"We have no vacancies, madam, I'm afraid. We're fully booked."

I recognised his voice from the phone call.

"I'm Melissa May. You called me earlier about my husband's belongings."

He gasped and touched his parted lips with his fingertips, suddenly interested as he looked me up and down.

"Ah, yes, Mrs May. We packed your husband's things. There wasn't much except for a few items of clothing and a briefcase. Our cleaner found his mobile phone tangled in the bed sheets, but the police may want that. They asked earlier if I'd found his phone."

"I'll take it. I'm going to the station right now."

He hesitated. "Well, if you're sure."

He went back through the door behind him and returned with Gavin's overnight bag and briefcase, placing them both on the counter. Then he took Gavin's phone out of his trouser pocket.

"Thank you," I said, throwing the phone into the bag.

"It was such a shock last night," he continued, eyebrows raised, clearly fishing for a scoop.

I nodded, not giving him anything. "Right."

"I'm sure your husband didn't deserve the way they treated him, like he was a common criminal. I told the officer that came to take his car away this morning that he'd always been a great guest. Been coming here for years, he has."

I smiled and nodded again. "Oh well, thanks for this." I held the bag and briefcase up as I backed out.

Unable to contain myself, I all but ran back to my car as fast as I could without drawing attention to myself. What a result. To be handed Gavin's phone was more than I could have dreamt of. Now I could wipe the GPS off both phones in case the police wanted to inspect it.

I headed for the motorway, making an effort to keep to the speed limit. The last thing I wanted was to be stopped by the police. I'd had my fill of police for one day.

At the same layby I'd launched Gavin's key last night, I rummaged around in his bag for the phone.

At first, in my haste, I couldn't work out how to delete the app. It turned out to be as simple as holding my finger down on the icon until it wobbled and then pressing the x.

Gone.

Then I deleted the app off my phone and sighed.

Guilty thoughts about Gavin kept niggling at me. I tried to ignore them, but they were getting stronger and stronger.

I'd made a mistake.

Poor Gavin would be locked up for a long, long time because of me. I would be without my husband for the first time in thirty years. My daughters were going to have to face the awful truth about their beloved father.

I'd wanted to protect them from the real truth but now we had the added scandal of murder.

The solution had seemed clear last night. Now, I wasn't so sure.

I'd have to build up the courage to call the station as soon as I got home. If this were happening for real, I would have phoned the police by now, desperate to know what my husband had been up to and why my house had been searched.

Nobody had the faintest idea I'd been involved. But I was terrified they'd be able to tell everything from my voice, that they'd ignore all the evidence pointing to Gavin and instead accuse me of being the killer.

***

They had Gavin May bang to rights.

He denied everything, of course, but gave no explanation.

His car was locked with no sign of forced entry, and the keys had still been in his possession. He admitted being the last person to see Carl Pilkington and Joe Bates before they were killed. He also had the murder weapon in his car. He admitted owning the cap described by witnesses, but denied any knowledge of how it got in his car.

It was cut and dried in every sense of the word, yet something didn't feel right to Adam.

Frances said he'd lost his marbles and he understood why, but his intuition had never failed him. Any time he'd ignored his inner voice in the past he always regretted it.

However, he had no choice but to charge Gavin May with three counts of murder. May would be held in custody until a court appearance on Monday morning.

The press was having a field day. Gavin had been granted name suppression until Monday, but it would-n't take long before everyone knew his identity.

Once charged, May tried to contact his wife, but couldn't get an answer at their home number. He left a message that tore at Adam's emotions. This guy, alt-hough troubled and confused in his private life, loved his family, of that Adam was certain. He seemed more concerned about what the scandal would do to his wife and daughters than what he faced himself.

Back at the office, Adam checked his messages. Melissa May had left three messages for him. He final-ised a few things before calling her back

"Mrs May?"

"Speaking."

"DI Stanley here, I got your messages."

"Detective, thank God. I demand you tell me what's happening with my husband. It's been a whole day and I expected him home by now. But instead he left a message telling me he's being held until Monday. What could be so bad you need to keep him locked up?"

Adam waited for her tirade to stop.

"Your husband has been charged with murder, Mrs May."

"Murder! Are you having a laugh?"

"He will be remanded in custody over the weekend, he's due in court on Monday," he said.

"You've made a terrible mistake. Who's he supposed to have murdered?" Her voice had gone up a few octaves.

"I really shouldn't say anymore."

"Can I see him?"

"I'm afraid not. At least not before Monday. I suggest you contact his solicitor; he'll be able to fill you in.

***

I couldn't stop playing Gavin's answerphone message over and over.

"Mel, it's me. Don't worry, I'm fine and just need you and the girls to know how much I love you. Whatever they told you, it's not true—not a word. Stay strong and calm, baby. I'll speak to you on Monday."

Listening to the devastation in his voice, I felt as though every breath was being squeezed out of me, and my heart broke.

I had called the station when I got home, hoping to be able to talk to him, but they forwarded my calls to the detective in charge who returned my call a while later without giving much away.

I wasn't sure whether or not I would be allowed in court on Monday, or whether I wanted to go. However, wild horses wouldn't keep Gavin's *innocent* wife away, so I didn't have much choice. Plus, I did want to see him. He sounded broken on the message and I needed to check he was okay.

I regretted my actions now. My mother had instigated everything, and without her I could see things much clearer. I should have given Gavin a chance to stop. Maybe if I'd threatened to tell somebody what he was doing, he might have stopped. But instead, I chose to be a cold-blooded killer, and now Gavin would pay the price.

I had very little guilt, or any feelings either way, for the dead men. The fact that their wives and children were saved from contracting a deadly disease made me certain what I'd done to them was justified.

However, an immense sadness gripped me when I thought about the devastation I'd caused to my own family.

Sitting at the kitchen table with my thoughts, a strange tinkling sound came from my handbag.

Gavin's phone lit up, making a different sound to his usual ring or text tone.

My stomach fluttered. I unlocked the phone and a tiny black message in the middle of the screen said: New Message. Nothing more. I wasn't used to the phone and didn't know what to do. I tapped my finger on the message and it seemed to have the desired effect. Another screen opened and asked for a username and password.

I had no idea what Gavin's username would be.

I tried—Gavin—and the standard pin number he used for most things, but the phone beeped at me and said incorrect username. I hoped that meant the pin was correct.

I tried another.

GavinMay

Incorrect username.

gavinmay

Incorrect username.

Melissa

Incorrect username.

MelissaMay

You have exceeded your login attempts. Try again after 60 minutes.

That stopped me. I would have been there all night if not. I had no clue what Gavin might use as a username—he'd never been a very imaginative man so his name or mine were the obvious choices.

I opened another couple of apps, but nothing told me very much of anything. Just as I was about to give up I found a Facebook account which I didn't know he had. His username—May Pole.

Intrigued by the message, and desperate to find what it was, I still had another forty-five minutes to wait before I could try the username again.

I contemplated ringing the girls to inform them of everything. It would be terrible for them to find out on the news. However, I couldn't face it right now.

I poured myself a large brandy and sipped at it, enjoying the fiery effect as it hit my stomach. The results were almost instantaneous, maybe because I hadn't eaten a proper meal in days. A heavy weakness spread through my limbs.

I jumped as Gavin's phone played the strange jingle once more, another message. Now I knew why he always had his phone on silent when he came home. I never understood it before.

I had no way of knowing if a second message had come through or if it was just a reminder for the first.

I felt I would go demented if I had to sit there waiting for the clock to tick around to the hour mark. So I topped my glass up and made myself a plate of crackers and cheese, surprised how hungry I was all of a sudden.

Food devoured, and armed with Dutch courage, I dialled Yvonne's number. I didn't know if she'd be home at seven o'clock on a Friday night, but I tried anyway.

Keith answered.

"Hi Keith, it's Mel."

"And how is my favourite mother-in-law?" He'd said the same thing to me for the past four years and we always had a bit of banter. But not tonight.

"Not the best, love. I need to speak to Vonny, is she there?"

"I'll get her for you." The smile had gone from his voice.

Yvonne sounded concerned when she answered the phone.

"What's wrong, Mum?"

I sighed. "There's something I need to tell you."

"Mum?"

I had to be very careful what I told her as I had only been told a tiny bit of it myself.

"Your dad's been arrested."

"Why? What for?"

"I don't know much myself. He stayed away last night and they arrested him in his motel room. Loads of police came here today to search the house. They had a warrant."

A sharp intake of breath was the only sound I heard.

"I spoke to the detective in charge and he told me Dad has been accused of murder."

There was nothing but silence at the other end of the phone and I began to think we'd been cut off.

"Yvonne?"

"I'm here, Mum. I just ..."

"I know, love. I feel the same myself."

"Who? And why? It doesn't make sense," she said.

"I don't know. I intended to contact Dad's solicitor, but I couldn't face it."

"Keith will do it. He understands all the jargon and procedures. He'll ask the right questions."

I'd forgotten Keith was a legal executive. He mainly dealt with residential and commercial conveyancing, but he'd have more of an idea than either of us.

"Oh, if he would, that will be a huge help."

"Did you tell Stella yet?"

"No, I've told nobody but you. I'll call her soon."

"I'll do it. You sit tight, Mum. We're on our way over."

"Oh gosh, no. I couldn't put you out like that," I said.

"Nonsense. We'll be late, but I have my key. We had no plans for the weekend anyway, so Keith can come too and then he can come home on Sunday. I'm due some time off from work and this is a family crisis. They'll be fine about it."

"Don't tell them!" I cried.

"Of course I won't tell anybody anything. Right, is Dad's solicitor the same one he's had for years? The guy in Godalming?"

"Yes, that's right. Terry Hamlett."

"Okay, I'll see you later then. And don't worry, I'm sure this is all a huge mistake."

"I hope so, Vonny, I really do."

After hanging up the phone, I raced to Yvonne's bedroom to pull out the duvet from underneath the bed. I found it folded on *top* of the bed. The police must have found it during the search. They probably thought it was a child's room, as the pink decor hadn't been changed for years. So they wouldn't have thought it too strange to find a duvet and pillow to be made up underneath the bed.

I tidied the room and made the bed.

Back in the kitchen, I remembered Gavin's phone. I typed May Pole as the username, followed by Gavin's usual password.

It took a few seconds of a wheel spinning on the screen before it opened up to a different page.

In the top corner of the screen was a photograph of Gavin looking very handsome. The site heading caused a rush of blood to my head and made me feel physically sick.

Married Yet Bi (for guys)

Discreet site for bisexual and bi-curious married men. Giving like-minded guys the chance to connect.

Down the side of the page, there were several tags.

Profile

Images

Inbox

Search Database

Search bi men in your immediate area

I clicked on profile.

Name - May Pole (Gavin).

Age – 48

The cheeky bastard had knocked six years off his age.

About May Pole (Gavin) - I am happily married, yet I have always been aware of my bisexuality. I love meeting up with men in a similar situation for sex—NO STRINGS.

The phone beeped and I almost dropped it. The battery light flashed so I took it through to the bedroom and plugged the phone into Gavin's charger at the side of his bed.

My heart was racing. It surprised me how sneaky and underhanded I felt for prying.

The house phone rang and I ran to answer it.

"Mum, Vonny's just told me. I can't believe it," wailed my youngest daughter Stella.

"It's okay, love. Don't upset yourself."

"I'll come over, but I won't get there until Sunday."

"Stella, listen to me. There's nothing you can do. I appreciate you wanting to be here, but honestly it's just a massive expense and inconvenience that you don't need right now. Let's just see what happens next week shall we?"

"But ..."

"Enough. Promise me."

"I'll wait until Monday and then if it's not sorted, I'm coming. End of story."

"We'll see." I sighed. "He might even be home by Monday."

"I hope so."

"Okay love, I'd best be off. I've got no bread or milk in for when Vonny gets here, so I'd best run to the shop before it closes."

Chapter 21

"So what will you do?" Amanda asked, glancing over her shoulder as a rowdy gang of blokes entered the bar.

Adam shrugged. "Not a lot without evidence. It's not looking good for the guy."

"You were the only person to believe in me, even when I doubted myself, you never wavered."

"At least the evidence in your case was only circumstantial. This one has every piece of evidence neatly placed for us to find. It's too tidy, too ..." he clicked his fingers three times, "... perfect."

"I'm aware you're not supposed to discuss the details, but I am a good listener."

Adam sighed. "I'm sorry, I'm not very good company, am I?"

"Don't be silly, there's a lot on your mind. It's not like you have an office job you can leave behind on a Friday afternoon and not think about until Monday morning."

Adam nodded.

"This is a man's future we're talking about. If you didn't give a toss, you wouldn't be you, and for your information—I quite like you." She blushed, and began tapping a bar mat on the table.

"Thanks. You're not so bad yourself." Adam reached for her hand and took the mat from her fingers. Their eyes met and they both chuckled.

"What does your partner think?"

"Who, Frances? Yeah, she's a good detective, but everything is black and white with her sometimes. She sees what she wants to see—if we have the evidence and the motive, we must have the perpetrator." He shrugged. "I never take things as gospel. There are a lot of master criminals out there who go to extreme lengths to convince us of their lies and half-truths."

"You should go with your gut. If not for you, that nasty Kate King would have had me locked up for the rest of my natural life. If you say he didn't commit the murders, I believe you."

Kate King had been DI when Adam first moved to London. He initially worked for the missing persons department, having had his fill of homicide. He met Amanda whilst searching for her father, Dennis Kidd, and was subsequently roped into the murder investigation. Kate had been medicalled out after a leg injury and Adam took her job.

"Thanks, Mand, I appreciate your confidence. Now, I just have to convince everybody else."

Adam sat up straight and shook his head and shoulders. "Right, enough of this, let's change the subject. How's the family?"

He felt guilty. They'd planned to go for a bite to eat and then on to a show. However, when they arrived in the West End, Amanda picked up on the fact that Adam wasn't in the mood and insisted they go for a quiet drink instead. The last thing he wanted to do was bore her rigid with his work woes, but he couldn't get Gavin May out of his head. He hated it when a case got under his skin like this one had, making it impossible for him to function normally, no matter what he tried to do. He should be making an effort with Amanda—after all, he'd been waiting all week to spend his night off with her.

"They're good, except Emma has been a little tyke recently. She's too clever for her own good, and a real little madam. I'll be glad when she's in full-time school, maybe she'll calm down a bit if she's tired."

Adam chuckled. "I wonder who she gets that off," he said, shaking his head and holding his hands up in a shrug.

"Cheeky." Amanda swatted at his arm. "I wasn't a bit like her growing up. I had to be a well-behaved little girl, and wouldn't dream of answering back." Her smile faded and then dropped.

Adam knew she was remembering her own childhood. He placed his hand on her thigh. "Does the fact they're all dead make things a little easier?"

She shrugged one shoulder. "In a lot of ways, yes. I'm not as paranoid anymore. I can pretend I'm normal, but every now and then, a word or a smell will trigger a memory and I'm right back there, a petrified little girl."

The mood had well and truly dampened down. Adam had an idea.

"What time do you need to be home by?" he asked.

Amanda laughed. "I'm not on a curfew."

Adam rolled his eyes. "I meant, what time does Sandra expect you back?"

"I know what you meant." She smiled. "Sandra's staying over."

Adam raised his eyebrows and then wiggled them.

"Why?" she asked, still smiling.

"Fancy grabbing a takeaway and going back to mine for a while?"

"I'd love to. I have a confession to make ..." She screwed up her face. "... I'm not really into going out all the time. I much prefer snuggling up on the sofa with a glass of wine and some nice company."

"We'll stop at the off-license on the way. And if we play our cards right, we could be snuggled on the sofa watching the 8-o'clock movie."

"Oooh, heaven," she giggled.

***

Amanda leaned over the top of the handbrake, kissing Adam on the cheek. "Thanks for a lovely night," she said. "You'd best get home, or you'll be dog tired tomorrow." She found the spicy mixture of his aftershave and natural manly scent intoxicating, and would love nothing more than to drag him down the path and up the stairs to her bed.

"And we'll all know who's to blame when I fall asleep at my desk." He laughed.

"Don't go blaming me, you cheeky bugger." She gave him a playful tap. "I told you hours ago we needed to call it a night."

"I was enjoying your company too much. Do you know, you're the first person to visit the flat since I moved to town?"

"Really?"

"Yeah, why sound so surprised? I only go back there myself to crash out."

"It's very tidy, considering you're never home. I'm impressed."

"Don't be. I pay the old woman next door to clean for me once a week. What? Don't look at me like that." He snorted, his hands in the air.

"Bugger! I think we've been busted." Amanda stared at the house.

Adam turned as the bedroom curtain closed. "Ooh! You're in big trouble now."

"Right you, scram." She straightened her cobalt blue sweater and opened the door. "Call me," she whispered before scurrying up the path.

The night air seemed much milder than earlier, yet Amanda shuddered. The feeling of being watched was much stronger again lately. She wasn't frightened like she used to be—she knew Andrew meant her no harm. It never failed to amaze her how she could sense him like this, but not have a clue where he was hiding.

She opened the front door and waved to Adam, who drove off down the street at a crawl.

Chapter 22

I woke with a start, disorientated. Then my eyes began to make out the shapes in the lounge. My heart hammered in my chest. What the hell had woken me?

"Gavin?" I called, my voice was wobbly and weak.

The lounge door burst open and my stomach lurched. Yvonne and Keith bustled into the room, their arms laden with bags and coats.

"Oh, Mum. You didn't need to wait up for us."

"I wasn't, I must have fallen asleep." I jumped up and helped them with their things. "Jesus, Yvonne, how long are you intending to stay?"

"For however long you need me." She met and held my gaze.

I almost protested. Instead, my eyes filled with the first tears of the day.

"Oh, Mum!" Vonny dropped everything and pulled me into her arms, where I allowed the tears free reign.

Keith looked embarrassed and clearly didn't know what to do. So he did what all English men and woman seem to do in a crisis—went to brew a pot of tea.

After a few minutes, I regained control and between us, Vonny and I organised the pile of stuff they'd brought with them. Two suitcases were placed next to the staircase ready for them to take up when they went to bed.

The rest of the things were for the kitchen, bags and bags of groceries. I presumed Stella told Vonny I didn't have anything in as she'd never brought groceries before. The house was usually well stocked, always had been.

Everything put away and the tea made, we sat at the kitchen table.

"Keith managed to get the day off on Monday so he can go to court," Yvonne said.

I nodded. "Thank you." I glanced at him.

"No problem." His smile didn't reach his eyes.

"We'll get to the bottom of this, Mum. There's got to be some mistake and the police will realise that."

I shrugged and looked away.

"Mum? What are you not telling us?" Vonny grasped my fingers on top of the table.

"Not now. I'm exhausted. I promise I'll explain everything in the morning."

"But ..."

Keith got to his feet and shook his head, cutting her off.

"Come on. It's late," I said, standing up.

I spent a few minutes washing the cups and straightening the cushions on the sofa before heading to my room, exhausted.

I climbed onto the bed, needing to crawl underneath instead, but paranoid Vonny would march in, in the morning, and catch me out.

I lay in the dark, my mind retracing every little thing over and over, eventually getting to the phone and Gavin's profile and my stomach turned in on itself.

What a fool I'd been for all these years.

I remembered I hadn't checked the message, too distracted by all the other information on the site.

I rolled over to Gavin's side and switched on the lamp. Then I unplugged his phone from the charger. My fingers were shaking so I took a deep breath and tried to calm myself.

Moments later, I'd logged into the site. A number 2 was flashing next to the message icon. I tapped the icon.

The inbox opened up. The first one said *Karravella has sent you a message*. I pressed my finger against the message and it too opened up.

Hi Gavin,

I'm in your neck of the woods again on Tuesday evening if you want to meet up? I won't have much time as the wife and kids will be at her parents, but I should be able to wangle half an hour or so.

We could meet at the same place at seven o'clock. Please confirm.
Brett

A sudden rage bubbled up within me—a seething hatred directed towards this man and the easy going way he tried to organise a sexual encounter with my husband. His poor family were probably already infected if they'd been meeting up often as the message insinuated.

I needed to know where they met, but couldn't ask Brett directly, it would surely set off warning bells.

I went back into the inbox and scrolled through heaps of messages until I found another from Karravella. This one was pretty much the same as the last so I continued searching and bingo!

Hi May pole,
I've read your profile and like what I see. I am interested in meeting up next Tuesday if you're available. My window is very tight (pardon the pun) as I'm only in the area for the evening while we visit family.
I could make the toilet block in Parswood Park at six o'clock.
Please confirm.
Brett

My stress levels hit amazing new heights. Gavin had told me he'd been careful and choosy. Meeting strangers in toilets didn't sound any of those things to me. It was sleazy and sordid.

I found my way back to the most recent message and hit reply.

Hi Brett,
See you there.
Gavin

Whether or not I would turn up was anybody's guess, but I had almost four days to decide.

***

Completely drained, I didn't have the energy to check the second message. My whole nervous system jangled, I felt I was close to toppling over the edge.

I put the phone back on the charger and snuggled down under the duvet, shutting out the world.

Feelings from my childhood returned with a vengeance as I thought about ending it all, about clos-ing my eyes for the last time and not having to deal with any more of this shit.

But then, images of Vonny and Stella swam into my mind and I knew I'd never put them through that. The truth about their dad would soon be made public and I needed to be there for them.

I slid off the bed and crawled underneath dragging the duvet with me. I craved sleep. My brain needed to switch off before my head exploded and then I would be no use to anybody.

"Mum?" Vonny called from the bedroom door.

I held my breath and waited for her to leave.

"Keith! Mum's not here." Her voice sounded close on hysterical.

The door opened wider and Keith entered the room. I could see his tan sheepskin slippers.

"She can't be far, her handbag's here."

"Mum?" Vonny's voice now came from down the hall.

Keith followed her.

I eased myself out from underneath the bed and padded down the hallway behind them, past the lounge, through the kitchen and out of the back door. I sat on the doorstep.

Moments later I heard someone at the kitchen sink. I opened the door and entered, shivering.

"Oh, there you are," Vonny said, placing her hand in the centre of her chest.

"Why? Where did you think I was?"

"I didn't know. I searched the house and couldn't find you."

"I popped out for a bit of fresh air, but it's freezing out there." My teeth chattered. The weather had been mild for the time of year, but today, the icy chill in the air felt like snow.

"Fancy going out in your night dress. Come and sit down, I'll make you a cup of tea and then you can tell me what's been happening."

"I'll have coffee, please, and then a shower. Believe me, what I've got to tell you can wait."

"For God's sake, Mother. I didn't sleep a wink thinking about what you had to tell me. The truth can't be any worse that the things I've imagined all night."

"We'll see about that, shall we?" I muttered.

Yvonne placed a cup of coffee in front of me and eyeballed me.

"What's that look for?" I snapped.

"You're not being fair. You need to tell me, Mum." Her lips were in a tight pout.

I took a deep breath and gazed at the ceiling as I exhaled in a controlled blow. Where should I begin?

"Things haven't been right for a while now."

"How'd you mean?" she said.

Keith walked into the kitchen and stopped. "Do you want me to leave?" he asked.

I shook my head. "No, sit down, Keith. You need to hear this too."

They both sat opposite me and they held hands on top of the table.

I placed my head in my hands and rubbed at my face. Both pairs of eyes stared at me, hardly blinking, as I battled with what to tell them.

"Were you and Dad splitting up?" she asked.

"No." I closed my eyes and sighed. I hated that I was about to shatter the illusion of her perfect family. "I found out recently ..." My mouth felt so dry I struggled to swallow my saliva.

"Go on."

"I found out, your father ..."

"What, just tell me, Mum."

"He's HIV positive."

Yvonne snatched her hand from Keith's and covered her mouth. Keith's eyes darted from me to Yvonne, repeatedly. The silence was deafening.

Yvonne's head shook in tiny movements as she tried to process my words.

"I didn't want to tell you, but I'm not sure how much will be made public now," I said, gutted for hurting her like this.

"I ... I don't understand," she said. "How?"

I raised my eyebrows at her.

"Dad wouldn't ... wouldn't ... Would he?"

My tight lips confirmed what she was denying.

Her eyes took on a pleading, confused look as she tried to make sense of the information presented to her.

"It's more awful than you're imagining. I'm sorry, but if you want the truth you'd better brace yourself," I said, feeling frazzled. I rubbed at my eyes before placing my hands together, as though praying, in front of my lips. I closed my eyes, dreading the words that were sure to make everything real once uttered.

Yvonne nodded to me as I opened my eyes.

I blew out, steadily. "Your dad is bi-sexual. He's been seeing men all over the country for years without my knowledge."

I witnessed the exact moment the realisation dawned on her.

"Mum, are you ...?" She couldn't go on.

I knew what she meant.

I wished I could shake my head, deny everything, but I couldn't. She needed to be told everything. Well, within reason.

"Yes. I am also HIV positive."

The guttural sounds Yvonne made tore the heart out of me. I couldn't stand any more. I left Keith comforting his wife and escaped to my bedroom.

An hour or so later, Yvonne seemed to have settled down. Although her eyes were still red and swollen, she'd stopped crying.

I hugged her and kissed the top of her head.

"Oh, Mum ..."

I placed my finger on her lips. "Shush. I'm okay. Honestly I am. There are drugs to help keep the illness at bay, nowadays." I suddenly remembered Gavin's medication and my breath hitched.

"What?" she said.

"Your dad's tablets—he hasn't got them with him."

"Can they wait until tomorrow? We can take them with us to the court," Keith said.

I shrugged. "I guess so." I smiled at Keith and touched his shoulder before sitting down.

"I rang Stella. She and Tina are on their way," Yvonne said.

"Oh no," I cried.

"She has a right to know, and what if the whole story comes out on Monday—we need to tell her first."

"She doesn't need to come all this way." I shook my head.

"She wants to, Mum. Just let us support you for once in your life." Yvonne argued. "We need to show the world that we're solid. No matter what happens now, we are family and will deal with this together."

"But what if your dad is found guilty of murder?" I said.

"Nonsense. I don't believe he's guilty for one minute—do you?"

I shook my head. "No. But I also wouldn't have believed everything else I now know to be true, this time last month."

Yvonne thought about it for a few minutes. Keith placed his arm around her shoulders, but she shrugged him off. "I still don't believe it and I can't see how any of this is connected," she said.

"Maybe it isn't, but it would be foolish to rule anything out at this stage."

Chapter 23

On Sunday, Stella, Tina and their spoiled, black standard poodle, Claude, arrived and my home was turned into a madhouse.

Yvonne took control of everything, leaving me to hide away in my room for hours on end. Mum made an appearance at the exact moment I thought my head might spin off with all the noise in the house.

Stella wasn't coping with the murder charges and had almost blown a gasket when Yvonne informed her of the HIV. She had always been noisy—everything she did had to be made into a huge performance. Her partner, Tina, tried to calm her, but even she couldn't manage it.

After listening to her wails and moans for over an hour, I'd had enough. I jumped off the bed and headed for the door.

Give her a break, Melissa. Imagine how you'd have been if this had happened to your precious father.

I stopped in my tracks. "Don't judge me—you've not even been around for days."

I've been here the whole time.

I sat back down on the bed. "It's difficult having a houseful when all this is going on."

They're here because they care, to support you.

"Do you think I don't know that?"

Give them a chance to get used to everything— you've had weeks, they've not.

"What makes you an expert all of a sudden?" I hissed.

On Monday morning, we all piled into Keith's SUV and headed to the court. Keith contacted Gavin's solicitor before we left. He warned him it was unlikely Gavin would be granted bail.

I dreaded seeing him. Prayed he wouldn't work everything out as soon as he clapped eyes on me, I'd never been good at keeping secrets from him.

When we arrived, the girls took one arm each and propelled me towards the courthouse.

I got through the security scanner without any hassle. Stella was asked to take off her leather jacket with the metal buttons and Keith had to remove his belt before they were cleared.

They hustled me inside the courtroom, my legs threatening to give out.

We sat on a wooden bench seat and I noticed the look that passed between Vonny and Stella as I shook uncontrollably.

Moments later, the courtroom filled and Gavin came in, handcuffed to a guard.

My heart almost stopped.

He didn't acknowledge us.

Stella called out and his back stiffened, but he continued to stare down at his feet.

I couldn't understand what was being said. It sounded like a solid hum of noise to me, and it took all my energy not to scramble over the top of everyone and get the hell out.

Within minutes, Gavin turned and was led from the courtroom. Yvonne and Stella were crying. I wasn't sure what had just happened, but I knew it wasn't good.

They ushered me back into the corridor. I was completely confused.

"What just happened, Keith?"

"The case has to go to trial because Gavin pleaded not guilty. He's been remanded in custody due to the seriousness of the crimes."

"What does that mean?" I asked.

"He will be taken to prison. If you wait here, I'll go and ask if we can see him." Keith walked off.

The three girls were huddled together. Tina had her arms around the other two. I stood to the side like a spare part, aware I should be crying too, but I couldn't.

Keith came back, his forehead furrowed.

"What's wrong?" I asked.

"We can visit him for a few minutes. However, he told his solicitor he doesn't want Vonny and Stella to go in." He smiled and shrugged an apology at the girls.

"Why ever not?" Stella's squealing voice hurt my ears.

Keith shook his head.

"He can't do that! We've come all this way to see him." She continued.

"For goodness sake, Stella, be bloody quiet for five minutes, will you? I can't hear myself think," I said.

"Mum!" Yvonne sounded shocked.

"Well, it's not all about her. He obviously feels terrible. Did you see the state of him?" My voice shook, along with the rest of me, and I felt light headed.

Keith put his arm around me and led me away.

We took the lift to the basement. As the doors opened, I panicked.

"I can't, Keith. I can't." I uncurled his fingers from my arm and shoved him in the direction of the stark white-washed corridor beyond.

"He's waiting for you, Mel. Come on, you'll be okay, I promise."

I took a deep breath and allowed him to guide me out of the lift.

The distinct lack of windows freaked me out, making me feel claustrophobic. I clawed at my neck, dragging the fine lace scarf off and poked it into my bag.

Fluorescent lights threatened to cause one of my migraines. Squinting, I turned my face towards Keith, who held me to his chest protectively.

Moments later a guard appeared and unlocked a huge white-painted metal door. Keith guided me through it and my breath hitched at the sight of Gavin sitting at a table in the middle of the room.

He gasped. I could tell he, too, was fighting back the tears.

My heart contracted. I took in the broken demeanour of my usually confident and larger than life husband—from his stooped shoulders to his sallow grey complexion. His raggedy five-o-clock shadow looked as though he'd used a knife and fork to shave with. However, the weight loss shocked me more than anything. What the hell had I done?

What you had to do.

I wasn't so sure. Another woman would have left home or kicked him out. Not take the law into her own hands, murdering people in cold blood, and setting her husband up to take the fall.

Don't go losing your nerve now.

I noticed both Gavin and Keith staring at me and I felt uncomfortable. What had just happened?

"What?" I asked, confused.

"I asked how you are." Gavin half smiled.

I nodded. "Okay, I think." I glanced around and shuddered. "You?"

He shrugged. "Coping. I prayed for a miracle today, for the judge to take pity on me and allow bail. But Terry told me there was no chance."

I couldn't talk. Couldn't think of a single thing to say.

"How are the girls?" Gavin asked.

I nodded and tried, without success, to swallow the lump in my throat.

"Upset and confused, but okay," Keith said when I didn't answer.

"They do believe I'm innocent, don't they?"

"Yeah, course they do, Gavin," Keith continued.

"Why do the police think you did it?" I asked.

Gavin scrubbed his face with his hands. "That's the odd thing. I was one of the last people to see each of the dead men. The murder weapon from two of the murders was found in my car and my car *was* the final murder weapon."

Shocked, Keith gasped and began to cough. He stood and left the room seeming to be choking to death.

"You believe me, don't you, Mel?"

"I don't know. I want to." My voice sounded flat.

He slumped in his chair as if all the air had been sucked out of him.

"I brought your medicine. What should I do with it?"

Gavin shrugged. "Dunno. Ask Terry."

"I'm sorry, Gavin. I wish I could say I believed you, but over the past few weeks I've learned nothing is as it seems with you."

"I know, but in this, I'm innocent."

"Not totally."

"What do you mean?"

"You chose to meet up with those men, and you chose to infect them."

"I'll hold my hands up. With the first two I admit, you're right. But that's all, I never hurt them, had no reason to."

"You never hurt them?" I felt like putting my hands around his throat and squeezing till every last bit of life seeped from him. "What about infecting their wives? Their children? Why can't you take responsibility for what you *have* done?"

He didn't respond. Just stared at me, his eyebrows knitted together and his mouth twisted.

I took a couple of deep breaths, replaying what had just been said. "The first two?" My stomach clenched.

"What?"

"You said you were guilty of having sex with the first two? What about the last one?"

Gavin shook his head. "He wasn't anything like that. It was strictly business."

A cry left my lips as I realised my mistake. Thoughts of that beautiful family all laughing in the car that day, followed by the vision of the twins' dad pinned to the wall, inches from my face—all these images swam around in my head.

I realised Keith had returned and was looking at me strangely. He spoke, but I couldn't hear the words. Gavin's mouth also moved. All I heard was a screaming white noise.

As Keith led me from the room, my eyes locked with Gavin's one last time and I knew the game was well and truly up.

Chapter 24

Two things horrified me. The first and most terrible of all, I'd killed an innocent man—torn a loving family apart. God only knows the damage I'd done to those beautiful little twins.

It never occurred to me that Gavin might have been working when he met those men. But of course he would have had a certain number of business meetings. Otherwise, the company wouldn't insist he stay away so often. They had an unmanned office in Pinevale where I had imagined those meetings would be conducted, not his motel room.

The noise playing in my ears sounded like an awful scream, which mirrored the way I felt.

At home, Keith all but carried me into my room and lay me on the bed, insisting the girls leave me alone. I was grateful. The awful sound had ceased, but I had my mum jabbering away instead.

It's not our fault. How were we to know?

We're talking about a man's life, Mother. Not just a whimsical decision that didn't mean anything—we should have checked and been absolutely certain first.

The second thing worrying me was Gavin. I thought he might work everything out if we were together long enough, and the expression on his face told me he had done just that. It was only a matter of time before the police came knocking.

You stupid, stupid girl. It was all going according to plan and you had to let it slip. You stupid, stupid girl.

"Enough!" I yelled. "I've had enough. Not one more fucking word out of you!"

The door burst open and Yvonne and Stella charged in the room. Keith and Tina stood in the doorway.

"Mum, what's wrong?" Yvonne cried.

"Get out!" I screamed. "Get out! Get out!" I continued as they backed out of the door, the horror evident on their faces.

They closed the door behind them.

I ran around the room in a fit of rage, upending the bookcase, swiping everything off the dressing table and kicking over the wicker chair, before collapsing onto the bed and tearing at my hair. All the while a guttural roar ripped from my throat.

Exhausted, all the suppressed emotions from the past weeks faded as I cried myself to sleep.

The sound of the phone ringing woke me from my slumber. Disorientated, I staggered from the bed thinking it was the middle of the night. The daylight peeking in through a chink in the curtains surprised me.

I opened the door a crack, hearing Keith talking on the phone. The tone of his voice intrigued me and I crept down the hallway towards him.

"That's bizarre. He was adamant he had nothing at all to do with the murders. No. No. He seemed fine, I think."

Keith's body tensed when he saw me, he screwed up his face in a troubled wince.

"Yes, I'll tell her. So what will happen now?" he continued.

"What?" I whispered.

He held one finger up and turned away from me.

The lounge door opened and Yvonne came into the hallway. I smiled at her and she smiled back with tight lips—not really a smile at all.

I shook my head and walked into the kitchen. Tina sat at the dining table reading a book. She closed the cover as I entered.

"Hi, Mel. You okay?"

"I'm tired, to be honest."

"Understandable, in the circumstances."

"I guess. How's Stella? Still sulking?"

"You know Stel, she'll have forgotten all about it by tea time."

I sighed and reached for the kettle.

Tina got to her feet. "Hey, let me do that. You sit down."

The shirt and trousers she'd worn to court had been replaced by a t-shirt and jeans. With her short-cropped brown hair and broad, chubby figure, she looked manlier than most men I knew. But she was a good girl, and a saint for putting up with my youngest daughter.

"Oh, you're okay, love. I need to do something. I might take Claude for a run in the park soon. I could do with a bit of fresh air." I got two mugs from the cupboard and raised one towards her.

She nodded.

"I was thinking the same myself. Shall we go together?" Her French accent, although mild, gave a sing-song lilt to her words.

"If you want, but to be honest I don't think I'm much company right now. I'd rather go alone if you don't mind."

"Well, if you're sure," she said.

I handed her a mug of coffee and rubbed her shoulder, then went in search of Keith. I'd expected him to come through by now. He'd been off the phone for ages.

I found him in the lounge with Stella and Yvonne. They all stopped talking as I entered.

"So what's happened now?" I asked.

They all looked stupidly at each other and then back at me.

"Keith. Tell me. Who was on the phone?"

"Terry Hamlet."

"Jesus, this is like pulling bloody teeth. Just spit it out."

"We don't want you upset, Mum," Yvonne said.

"A bit late for that, don't you think?" I smiled.

"But ..."

"Vonny, tell me what's happening, I'm okay, I promise."

Stella and Yvonne turned to Keith.

Keith cleared his throat. "Well, erm ... Terry said Gavin changed his plea."

"Meaning?" I shook my head, confused.

"Meaning ..." he swallowed, his Adam's apple bobbing up and down. "... meaning, he's confessed to all three murders."

"He can't have! He didn't do it!" I shook my head, scanning everyone's face in turn. None of them met my eyes.

The cool evening air was exactly what I needed. Claude trotted along beside me on his lead.

The thoughts churned around and around in my brain making me dizzy, and I just had to escape from all the sympathetic and wary gazes. You'd think I wouldn't care, considering they were family and experiencing the exact same feelings as me, but I couldn't cope.

Why had Gavin confessed? Although I knew he'd worked it out, I'd expected him to tell the police, or at least profess his innocence and hope like hell he got off. Now he was as good as fucked.

Works out better for you, wouldn't you say, girl?

I groaned. I'd wanted to escape everyone, forgetting one person was ever present.

Charming!

I shook my head and tugged at Claude's lead. "C'mon, boy," I said, breaking into a sprint.

I pushed hard for the first few minutes, but my energy soon flagged and I eased off to a slow jog. I used to run as a child, I was even on the cross country team at school, but hadn't needed to run in a long time.

Half an hour later I arrived home, exhilarated—knackered but exhilarated.

Claude looked like he was on the verge of collapse. I doubted he got much exercise at home in France. Their new apartment was on the seventh floor. The stairs were the only physical workout the poor mutt got. They led straight out onto the postage stamp lawn to do his business—which I thought was cruel. Yet they indulged the pampered pooch in other ways, treating it like a human being.

"Oh my God, what have you done to him?" Tina laughed as we fell in the front door. "What's your nana done to you, Claudie? Hey? Hey?" She dropped to her knees slobbering all over the poor dog, who wanted nothing more than a bowl of water and a lie-down.

"I think he'll sleep tonight No howling like last night." I hoped the smile would soften the edge to my voice.

"Aw, sorry. I didn't realise you heard him from the back of the house. He's not used to sleeping on his own."

"Why, who does he sleep with?" I asked, horrified.

"Me and Stel. He gets in our bed at home." She screwed her face up in a wince.

"That's your business, but I'm sorry, I'm being generous allowing him in the house at all. There's no chance I'll let him in the bedrooms." I shuddered.

I practically bounced through to the kitchen, more energetic than I'd felt in ages. Yvonne stood at the stove stirring something in a huge pan. Stella sat at the table wiping her eyes.

"You look a bit better, Mum," Vonny said.

"Yeah, I feel it, to be honest. Did anything else happen while we were out?"

"No. Oh, except Keith went home. He has meetings all week he can't get out of."

"You should have gone too. It's pointless us all sitting around here like Piffy on a rock bun," I said, glancing at Stella.

"Like what?" Yvonne laughed. Stella sobbed louder.

I shook my head and waved my hand in her direction as though wafting a fly. "Never mind."

It occurred to me that, although I adored my children, Stella irritated me to distraction. She'd always been harder to deal with than Yvonne, but we'd indulged that over the years. As the youngest, she got away with a lot. At the moment, not having a lot of energy to waste on people, I found Stella drained me more than anyone else.

She squinted her eyes. "What?" she said, defensively.

Realising my thoughts must be written all over my face, I shook my head. "Nothing." I turned away. "What you making, Vonny?"

"I've made a pan of soup. I know you don't like vegetables, before you start, Stel, but I'll blend yours. None of us have eaten all day."

I didn't much fancy eating soup myself, but she was right. We needed something nutritious inside us.

It felt nice to behave like an ordinary family. I sliced a white cobb loaf that Keith had bought before he left. Stella made a pot of tea and Tina fed Claude before laying the table.

The soup tasted delicious and we all ate with gusto, even Stella, who didn't like anything. It's surprising what even the fussiest person will eat when they're starving enough.

It didn't take too long before the conversation came back around to Gavin.

"I watched the news while you were out," Yvonne said.

I cocked my head backwards.

"They said a man from Surrey has pleaded guilty to three counts of murder, but they haven't named him yet. Keith said Terry's trying to push for name suppression, but he's unsure how long they'll agree to that."

"Hopefully long enough for us to get our own heads around it." I sighed.

"You could always come and stay with us for a while, Mum, if it did get out," Yvonne said.

I nodded. "We'll see."

A glance passed between Stella and Tina, but no offer of accommodation came forward. Stella was still obviously sulking.

"Thanks for the soup, Vonny. I'm going to have a lie down. Can I leave you with the dishes?" I asked, exhausted.

"I'll do them," Tina jumped up.

She's a good girl, they all were. I'd be sure to tell them all tomorrow.

A strange vibrating sound puzzled me when I entered the bedroom. I soon discovered it came from Gavin's phone. I'd switched the volume off on Friday after replying to the message. I didn't want the girls investigating a strange ringing in my room, unsure what they might discover.

There had been several alerts from the website. A couple of nudges and three winks, whatever that meant.

So long as they stick to nudges and winks they'll be safe.

I rolled my eyes. "We're not going to do anything else, Mum," I whispered.

We'll see.

***

Adam shook his head as he hung up the phone.

"Frances?" he called.

Frances appeared in his office doorway. "Yes, boss?"

"I just had the strangest phone call."

"Go on."

"Gavin May has confessed to three counts of murder."

"See, I told you. Did he confess in court?"

"No. That's the strange part. He pleaded not guilty, and then afterwards, called his solicitor wanting to change his plea." Adam shook his head again. "Something about this case doesn't add up."

"Don't tell me you still believe he's innocent?"

Adam shrugged. Confession or not, he didn't believe Gavin May. He needed to go through the evidence again.

Maybe he should have got forensics to examine the motel unit, but at the time they had all they needed. Plus, the killer hadn't got out of the vehicle—the witnesses confirmed that, so there would have been no real evidence inside the room.

The pipe wrench had blood on it from the first two victims. Gavin admitted seeing all three men before they were murdered and DNA confirmed he'd had sex with two of them.

One piece of evidence didn't fit. A single grey hair found inside the cap didn't belong to Gavin and the DNA didn't match anything on the database. However, that failed to prove anything. Somebody may have worn the cap before Gavin.

Now, with this confession, Adam knew he should let it go, but he couldn't. Something stank to high heaven with this case and he had the stench lodged firmly up his nose.

***

Adam arranged for him and Frances to see Gavin, who insisted his solicitor be present. Adam was unable to shake the feeling they were missing something.

Gavin's eyebrows furrowed as he shook his head, clearly puzzled by Adam. At the last interview, Adam had insisted he was guilty and Gavin vehemently denied it. Now, the situation was reversed.

"Why did you change your mind?" Adam asked.

"Because, I couldn't lie any longer."

"Bullshit! Then why didn't you admit it to your solicitor and make a deal before going to court—not after."

Gavin shrugged. "I thought I might get out on bail if I pleaded not guilty. Get to spend a bit of time with my wife and daughters."

"Why are you lying?"

"I'm not lying. I did it," Gavin's voice sounded calm, bored even. He pinched the spot in between his eyes, as though he had the beginnings of a headache.

"Tell me about the murders. The details please," Adam said.

"I had sex with Carl. Followed him home and we had a fight."

"How did you know him?" Adam said.

"I didn't. We met over the Internet." Gavin sighed.

"We searched your computer and found no record of this supposed website."

"I never used the home computer. I didn't want Mel finding out so I used my mobile."

Adam reached into his pocket and pulled out a notepad. "Write your username and password down for me, please."

Gavin hesitated before scribbling the details down.

"Thanks." Adam glanced at the looped handwriting before placing the pad back into his pocket. "Let's get back to Carl. What did you fight over?"

"I told him I was HIV positive. He went mad and we fought."

"How did he die?"

"He locked me in the van. I kicked the doors open and hit him with a wrench."

"This is utter crap, Gavin. You've repeated, word for word, what we told you last week."

Gavin shrugged again. "Turns out you were right all along then, doesn't it?"

"Who are you trying to protect?"

Gavin's face and neck flushed. "No one," he said, leaning forward suddenly, his eyes piercing Adam's.

Startled, Frances jumped back in her seat.

"Something doesn't add up, and I will get to the bottom of it," Adam said, shaking his head.

"You do that." Gavin's trembling top lip belied the conviction in his voice. He rubbed his throat.

Adam knew damn well Gavin wasn't guilty, but with all the evidence against him how could he prove it?

"Why did you kill Anthony Kingsley?"

This murder had been a mystery to them. There was no obvious reason Gavin would want Kingsley dead, and he was worth a lot of money to him alive—at least until the business deal had been finalised.

Gavin glanced at his solicitor and back to Adam for a few seconds, before focusing on his hands. "I didn't like him. He ... erm, he turned me down."

"You're saying you made sexual advances towards Mr Kingsley and he rejected you?"

Gavin nodded.

"Have you always been such a stud throughout your life, Mr May?" Frances piped up.

"What?" Gavin's eyes narrowed and his top lip curled.

"Well, it's par for the course to get turned down if you're actively seeking sexual partners. If we all went around killing everyone who spurned us, there wouldn't be anyone left in the world."

Another one-shouldered shrug.

Adam got to his feet. "That's all for now. But I can assure you, this is far from over. We'll be in touch."

Chapter 25

My bedroom door opened and closed again a few seconds later. The last few mornings I'd set the alarm clock, getting up before everybody so they wouldn't discover I slept underneath the bed.

"Shit!" I muttered as I crawled out. "I need to get a bloody lock put on the door."

I made the bed before venturing out to face the day and the girls.

Yvonne sat in the lounge—her phone pressed to her ear and she whispered into it.

I nodded to her and she waved.

Stella knelt on the kitchen floor by the back door, feeding Claude toast.

"What you doing?"

"Claudie isn't very well today. He wouldn't eat his niblets."

The dog opened his mouth pathetically, taking the toast offered.

"He looks fine to me." I sighed.

"He's had his pattern disrupted, haven't you, boy?"

"I didn't ask you to disrupt him. In fact, I remember quite the opposite being true. You can take him home for all I care."

"Why are you being so nasty?"

"I'm not nasty? I'm telling you I'm fine. If you want to go home, go!"

A slight twinge of guilt gripped me, I shrugged. "I appreciate you coming, of course I do, but I'm not good company at the moment. I'm not up to entertaining guests or having wonderful and meaningful mother and daughter chats because my life is in turmoil. I'm lashing out at you because my life is in turmoil. I want to be alone and to shut out the world because my life is in turmoil."

I snatched the tea-towel from the side and began wiping last night's dishes from the draining board.

Stella jumped up from the floor. "I'll do that. Why don't you go for a bath?"

She took the towel from me and I let the damp fabric slip from my grasp. She meant well, they all did. However, the irritability I felt continued to bubble away under the surface like a pressure cooker.

"I'll have a shower. Can you make me a coffee, please?" I smiled, trying to appease her.

"Course I will, how about some breakfast?"

"Coffee's fine for now, thanks."

I locked the bathroom door behind me. This seemed to be the only place I could be alone.

I glanced in the mirror.

Not quite. Mum's eyes flashed back at me.

You know what I mean.

We need to decide what we're going to do later.

Later?

Our date.

Oh no. I can't even think about that now.

You must. The man has already slept with Gavin, and he's got a wife and children.

Exactly, we're too late to help them.

Maybe, but what about all the others he will go on to infect. We're not talking about one or two partners—these disgusting creatures are promiscuous and will dip it into anyone and everyone they can.

"Enough!" I shouted. "You do it, I can't."

As you wish.

There was a tap on the door. "Mum, are you okay?" Yvonne asked.

"Fine," I snapped.

She and Stella began whispering to each other behind the door.

"Can't I have a shit in peace?" Mum yelled.

One of the girls gasped and I heard them retreat into the lounge, closing the door behind them.

"Mum!" I said.

Well, they need to learn.

"I know, but ..."

If I'm to do this—I need you to back off.

Showered and changed, I found the girls huddled together in the lounge.

Stella jumped up. "I'll do you another coffee, this one's cold," she said, picking up a cup from the table.

"Thanks." I sat on the armchair.

"We've been thinking, Mum," Yvonne said.

"Oh, yeah," I raised my eyebrows.

"We think you should see a doctor."

"I don't need a doctor." My voice came out higher pitched than usual.

"You've had an awful shock. What with the HIV and having to deal with dad's secret. But now you have this on top and we can tell you're not coping," she said.

"I'm coping."

"Mum, you're sleeping underneath your bed and you're talking to yourself. We're worried about you. Maybe the doctor can give you something to calm your nerves."

I took a deep breath. "I know you mean well, all of you." I glanced at Tina, who fidgeted in her seat, not able to look me in the eye. "But I'm okay. Yes, I'm behaving strangely, I'm tetchy and can't help taking everything out on you guys, but it's my way of coping right now. Which is why I think you should all go home."

Stella returned and placed a steaming cup of coffee in front of me.

"Thanks, love." I smiled.

"We're not leaving you, Mum. Not yet anyway," Yvonne said.

"You can't stay forever. You have your jobs, your own lives."

"I plan on leaving my job anyway, just as soon as I get pregnant. It's not as though we need the money. Keith earns plenty."

"And you need to be there for him. It's not fair Keith in Birmingham alone and you here."

"We're all right for a few weeks, Mum," Stella said. "We've got heaps of holidays we need to take."

"Okay, if that's the case, you might as well go home to Keith, Yvonne. You don't all need to be here at the same time, and if I still need the company once Stella and Tina go home, you can come back."

"I don't—"

"I know you want to help, but I'm fine. I don't want to put any of you out on my account. Nobody can do a thing until the trial."

"There'll be no trial now," Yvonne said. "Dad pleaded guilty so he won't need a trial—just a hearing and then sentencing. Keith just told me."

"When will that be?"

"Not long, maybe a week or two according to Keith," Yvonne said.

My head spun.

"I might go away for a while afterwards. The truth will be out by then, and I imagine the press will camp out on the doorstep," I said.

"Keith said we can visit Dad if we want. He's on remand so we don't need a visiting order," Stella said.

"I don't want to. I get too upset."

Stella grabbed my hand. "We'll go. We can take him some stuff. I'll check with the prison what he's allowed."

I nodded, uncurled her fingers from mine and reached for my coffee.

***

"Frances, I can't find the report from Gavin May's motel. I wanted to check if he went out again that night."

"There isn't one. They don't have an electronic system. Basic door locks and keys I'm afraid."

"Bugger."

"You need to let it go, Adam. Otherwise, you'll burn yourself out."

Adam had been working on another case all morning. A twenty-three-year-old Indian woman, strangled to death by her thirty-eight-year-old husband because she hadn't cooked his dinner on time. But he couldn't focus. Gavin May's case kept hijacking his mind.

A thought struck him. He leapt from his desk and sped from the room leaving Frances looking on with her mouth agape.

Downstairs in the basement, he located the evidence box for Gavin May.

Inside were several items. Only one of them interested him.

"Bingo."

He raced back up the stairs to his office and threw the clear plastic bag down on the desk in front of Frances.

"Look at that—tell me what you see."

She lifted the bag up and peered through the plastic to examine the contents.

"A cap."

He nodded. "And?"

She turned the bag over and back again, then shrugged. "I don't know."

"Look at the fastening."

Frances examined the cap again and her eyes lit up. "Oh, I see."

"It's set to the tightest fitting. Now I wouldn't say our Mr May has the biggest head I'd ever seen, but it's definitely bigger than that. I bet you'd even struggle to get it on."

Frances nodded. "So now what?" Are we looking for a youngster?"

"Or a woman. Don't forget the footprints on the inside of the van doors. They're not Gavin's."

Frances nodded again. "But there were no identifying marks on the footprints."

"Maybe not, but they were a size 5 not a size 9. We need to speak to Mrs May."

Almost two hours later, Adam and Frances pulled up outside the quaint dormer bungalow in Surrey.

Adam rapped on the lounge window with his keys after the knock on the door went unanswered.

A dog barked and then a small, grey-haired woman opened the door.

"Mrs May?" Adam said, holding up his badge.

She nodded, confusion flashing across her face.

"DI Adam Stanley and DS Holly Frances. Can we have a chat?"

She nodded and stepped backwards, allowing them to enter.

"Can I get you a cup of tea, Detectives?" she asked.

"That's kind of you. We've had a long drive and I'm parched," Adam said, bending slightly. Always conscious of his size in small spaces, he knew he intimidated people, so he tried to make himself appear ... less.

They followed her into the kitchen and she offered them a seat at the dining table.

Once she'd established how they took their tea, she filled the kettle and sat down herself.

"So what can I do for you, Detectives?"

"We are with the CID investigating your husband's case," Adam said.

She nodded.

"No doubt you're aware Gavin's confessed to all three murders."

She nodded again. "Yes, I was told."

"The thing is, Mrs May, we don't believe he's guilty."

Her eyebrows furrowed and her head snapped back. "Really?"

"What can you tell me about your husband, Mrs May?"

"Melissa, please. Erm ... He was always a good husband. We've been married for almost thirty years and never had any trouble until recently."

"Are you referring to the HIV?"

"Yes, I am."

"That must have been a terrible shock," Adam said.

Melissa glanced down at her hands and began picking at her thumbnail. "I was devastated," she whispered.

"If you don't mind me saying, Melissa, most woman would be long gone by now," Frances said. "Myself included. It takes a very special person to forgive their partner after thirty years of betrayal."

"He told you?" Melissa whispered.

Frances nodded.

"I haven't forgiven him," Melissa spat. "I didn't know what to do and I couldn't bear to think of my daughters finding out. I think he's disgusting."

Frances nodded and got up the finish the tea.

"Oh, thanks," Melissa said. "I had to tell them in the end. Everyone will know soon, won't they?"

"I'm afraid so." Adam nodded. She wasn't as old as he'd first thought, maybe late forties, early fifties. Her grey hair made him think she was much older when he first met her.

"If somebody told me last week that the HIV would be the least of our worries, I would have laughed in their face," Melissa said.

"I can imagine. What are your thoughts on the murders?"

"I'm still in shock. He's never been a violent man, always had the gift of the gab. He would, and could, talk himself out of any situation. Murder seems too far-fetched for him. I don't believe he's guilty."

Frances placed the cups on the table. "Can I use your bathroom, Mrs May?"

Melissa nodded, wrapping her hands around the cup. "Of course. It's the first door on the left past the staircase."

Frances left the room.

Melissa turned back to Adam. "Why did he confess if he's innocent?"

Adam shrugged.

"I've come to the conclusion, thirty long years or not, that I don't think I know my husband very well."

Once Frances returned, Adam pulled the plastic bag containing the cap from his jacket pocket. "Do you recognise this, Melissa?" He smiled.

She hesitated before taking the bag from him, nodding. "Yes, Gavin's cap."

"Did you ever wear it?"

She shook her head. "No, I ... oh, wait a minute, yes I did. We went to a firework display a while ago and Gavin insisted. Why?"

"No real reason." He smiled again.

They made small talk for a few minutes while he and Frances drank their tea.

"Thanks for your help, Melissa." Adam drained his cup and got up to leave. Frances did the same.

"One last thing, Melissa." Adam paused in the doorway. "Did you visit Gavin yet?"

She nodded. "At the court yesterday. My daughters are visiting him today."

"How did he seem?"

"Sad. Lost. I hated seeing him like that," she said. "It would be much easier if he were dead."

The front door shut behind them. Adam glanced at Frances as they walked to the car. "She did it."

"What? How do you know?" Frances screwed her face up, shaking her head.

"Trust me. I'm positive."

"She's too fragile. Surely she can't be strong enough to commit those murders?"

"Not necessarily, Frances. Adrenalin would kick in and provide the additional strength needed." They spoke over the top of the car.

Frances blew out her cheeks and bent to get into the passenger seat.

Adam slid in beside her and banged the heels of his hands on the steering wheel.

"What are you thinking?" Frances asked.

"Why else would Gavin change his plea straight after she saw him?"

"Guilt! Maybe she shamed him into confessing."

"Bullshit. He knows she did it and would rather take the rap than see her banged up."

"A bit hard to believe if you ask me, boss." She shrugged.

He exhaled as he leaned his head on the headrest. After a few silent minutes he sat up straight, shook himself and turned the key in the ignition.

"Right. We need to go back to the beginning, except this time we need *Mrs* May in the frame. She's bound to have slipped up somewhere," he said.

Adam pulled his car into the station car park, surprised they were back already. He glanced at Frances, who had been silent for most of the journey.

"Penny for them," he said.

"I'm still trying to get my head around what you said. I can't see how that little lady is capable of murder."

"Don't underestimate her, Frances. That's the worst mistake we could make."

"I'm not. She just seemed so normal."

"Think about what she's been through in the past few weeks—it's enough to rock anyone's world."

Frances nodded. "I guess. And I did notice a pair of size five shoes when I went to the toilet."

"I'm telling you, Frances. She's our killer."

"Okay then, first things first. We need to check her statement and verify her whereabouts at the time of each of the murders."

"Great, and I think I'll pay our Mr May another visit."

Chapter 26

Mum was getting way out of control. I'd almost died of heart failure when she blurted out Gavin should be dead. The huge detective bloke looked at me as though I'd stabbed him with a fork.

"You didn't need to say that, Mum!"

I was being honest. You should have bumped him off in the first place.

"Go away, Mother," I shouted.

After everything I've done, this is the thanks I get.

"I need to sleep." I shook my head, exhausted all of a sudden.

SLEEP THEN. WHO'S STOPPING YOU.

Her voice was so loud I thought my head might explode.

Claude howled.

And shut that fucking dog up!

I opened the back door and let Claude in. I'd put him outside when the detectives had first knocked.

Claude followed me through to the lounge and as I got on the sofa, he lay on the floor beside me.

I woke to the sounds of the girls arriving home. To my horror Claude lay on my chest. As I opened my eyes, he licked at my mouth. I almost gagged.

I shoved at the overgrown ape before anyone discovered him up on the sofa. After moaning all week that he wasn't allowed on the furniture, I'd never live it down.

The comical looking dog hit the floor like a sack of spuds, an indignant expression on his face.

The stirrings of a giggle began in my stomach. I tried my hardest to control myself, but it formed into a full on belly laugh. I hadn't laughed in such a long time. Tears filled my eyes and the girls found me half sobbing, half laughing.

"Oh no, Mum. What's happened?" Stella ran to me trying to pull me into her arms.

I shook my head and tried to push her away. She clearly thought I was crying, which made me laugh even harder.

Regaining control, I glanced at the girls and all three of them stood in front of me, their eyes wide and mouths agape.

"What the hell just happened?" Stella asked.

My shoulders began shaking again. My stomach spasmed, preventing me from breathing properly and a high pitched, unintelligible sound escaped me.

Stella realised I was laughing and spun away, leaving the room in obvious disgust. I figured the meeting with Gavin hadn't gone well. Stella's reaction made Tina and Yvonne crack up laughing and I had another uncontrollable fit of laughter.

Once we'd all calmed down, I wiped my eyes on the sleeve of my top. "How's your dad?"

"He wouldn't see us," Yvonne said.

"Doesn't surprise me after yesterday. He's a proud man and thinks the world of you girls."

"I understand. It stings though. Especially with him knowing how far we travelled today. He could have given us a couple of minutes. Stella's taken it badly,"

"We need to respect his wishes."

Yvonne nodded.

Tina went in search of Stella, but Claude stayed by my side.

"Are you gonna let me in on the joke?" Yvonne said.

I shook my head. My stomach bounced again as I replayed it in my mind. My breath came out like Muttley from The Wacky Races and I had to force myself to calm down.

"I woke up to find Claude on the sofa with me."

Her eyes opened so wide I thought they might pop. "Mother!"

"I didn't know, I was asleep. But it *was* funny."

Yvonne laughed. "Stella would insist he sleeps in bed with her if she knew."

"Which is why I launched the poor dog halfway across the room when I realised." I laughed.

"How did your day go?"

I considered telling her about my visitors, but changed my mind.

"Quiet, nothing to report. I had a good sleep and I feel a lot better, to be honest."

"I am glad. What do you fancy for dinner?"

I glanced at the clock—four-thirty.

"We're going for a walk later."

Claude sat up and began to growl.

"We?"

"Me and Claude, I meant." I smiled.

I opened the wardrobe door, looking to change my outfit.

Wear dark clothes.

I've got none.

You must own something, you're being awkward.

I'm being awkward! You had no right to speak to Vonny like that earlier. They already think I'm crackers without you talking about us as we.

We *are* we.

To us we are. Not to anyone else. Now we're gonna have to take the bloody dog with us and he can't stand you.

He'll give us a good reason to be in the park.

I shook my head as I pulled on a pair of dark blue jeans, a red jersey and short black boots. After rummaging about in the hall cupboard, I found a light-weight, navy blue anorak.

As I walked into the kitchen, Claude began to growl.

Piss off, Mother.

"Come on Claude, let's go for a walk." I pulled the anorak over my head, leaving the hood up.

"Is it going to rain, Mel?" Tina appeared behind me.

"Not sure, but best to be safe than sorry."

"I guess so. Claudie, what's wrong with you?"

"I don't think he likes my hood," I said. "Come on silly sausage. Shall we go for a run?"

Claude made a low continual rumbling sound.

"You're spoiling him you know, two big walks in a row. He doesn't get much exercise at home."

"Oh well, at least he slept last night. We both did." I clipped Claude's lead in place. He still grumbled at me.

Tina left the room.

Get a knife.

Claude barked.

Oh, Mum, be quiet. Claude can sense you're here.

Get a knife then, a big one.

I glanced over my shoulder to make sure I was still alone, and opened the utensil drawer. I found a medium sized knife, the blade approximately one inch wide and five inches long. I slid it up the sleeve of my anorak.

"Come on, boy." We slipped out the back door.

Although already dark, the stars were out in force, plus the street lights lit up the main walkways.

We walked to the park, approximately a mile or so away. I had no idea what I would do once we arrived, but the way I felt, it wouldn't be much.

You will have to be fast. No mucking around.

Claude yelped and whined, then looked up at me with huge brown eyes.

"You're okay, Claude."

I just want to check him out, Mum. Let's play it by ear, shall we?

I'm sure you live in la-la land, Melissa. You need to do this.

No, I don't. He's not my husband. I've done my duty and got Gavin off the streets.

But his disease is still rife. I'm sick and tired of arguing with you. I'll do what's needed.

The familiar shroud of numbness descended over me. It felt nice, comforting, like slipping into a pair of well-worn slippers. By the time we were halfway to the park, Mum was in total control.

***

Brett Graham had had one of those days when the universe seemed to be in cahoots with the devil, trying every little thing to prevent him being on time.

Caroline, his wife, woke up with a toothache and had been impossible all day. And today happened to be his only day off in a fortnight.

They had got married around ten years ago. Neither of them were happy anymore. Caroline was a domineering woman and he would have left her years ago if only he possessed a pair of balls. They also had their two children to consider, Sally aged nine and eight-year-old Tom.

Caroline and Sally, who clashed at the best of times, had a massive fight as soon as Sally arrived home from school.

Tom loved visiting his grandparents, but Sally, at that age where only mates are cool, said old people were boring and she didn't want to go to a fossil's birthday party. The cause of the argument.

Brett had been sat on the toilet, minding his own business, when the fight began. He cringed at Caroline's screeching, over-the-top voice. Half-way down the stairs, he heard a loud slap and Sally, sobbing her little heart out, ran past him and up to her room holding her hand to her face.

He didn't agree with smacking the children, but Caroline didn't listen. Her upbringing had been different from his. She insisted it never did her any harm, and couldn't see any problem with a short, sharp slap to the back of the legs or a swipe across the head. She made him feel sick.

After playing go-between for the best part of an hour, he convinced Sally to apologise to her mother for the sake of a quiet life. They gave each other a half-hearted hug before heading to the car, almost an hour later than planned.

And then, on the final leg of the hour long journey, they got a flat tyre.

He all but dragged Caroline and the kids out of the car when they arrived at Caroline's parents' house, then he drove across town like a madman.

Both he and Caroline grew up in the area and would often visit friends and family at separate times. Otherwise, they'd never get round them all.

Today he had an hour to get back before all the family arrived to sing happy birthday to the old fart.

Caroline thought he'd arranged to meet up with Harvey, his best friend from school. Harvey had recently split up with his wife and it had hit him hard. Caroline wasn't a great fan of Harvey and was more than happy for Brett to visit alone. The plan had been to visit Harvey *before* his meeting with Gavin. At least then, he'd have some real answers to Caroline's fifty questions on the way home. He wouldn't have time for that now. He was already running late.

Pulling his car up outside the main entrance to the park, he wandered in and towards the toilet block, a couple of minutes' walk from the gate.

As he approached, he expected to see Gavin standing around waiting for him, especially because he was a few minutes late himself, but Gavin was nowhere to be seen.

Brett shivered, wishing he'd grabbed his jacket from the car.

After checking Gavin wasn't waiting inside the gents, he stepped back outside and almost jumped out of his skin as a woman appeared. She was dressed in dark clothing and walking a jet black dog.

"Evening," he smiled. He was surprised a woman would be out in the park at night.

She smiled back and headed towards the ladies. The dog growled at him. He watched as she tied the lanky thing up to the bench outside.

Walking towards the main path, he glanced up and down. Maybe Gavin got sick of waiting and had already left, but he wasn't that late, ten minutes at the most.

He checked his phone as he turned back towards the toilet block and he came face to face with the same woman, minus the dog.

"Oh, sorry," he said, noticing the unnatural brightness of her eyes. Feeling an almighty punch to the chest, he staggered backwards a few steps.

It seemed as though the world had slowed to a fraction of its usual speed. The woman stood still, unmoving, staring with those strange bright eyes.

He glanced down. He couldn't work out what was protruding from his chest. He reached up and touched it as his knees gave way, and he sank to the ground.

He glanced back at the strange unmoving woman. As he felt the life ooze from him, he saw her smile.

Chapter 27

Gavin May seemed even more on edge than yesterday. One leg crossed over the other, twitching continually, and he chewed on his thumb-nail.

He sighed as Adam walked into the room.

"What now? I've told you everything. What more do you want from me?"

"You and I both know that's utter crap, Gavin." Adam took a seat opposite him in the small room.

A prison officer stood behind Gavin, to the side of the door.

Gavin's eyes flickered before refocusing and settling on Adam's steady gaze.

"Are you sure you don't want your solicitor present?" Adam asked.

"Positive, thanks."

"I've just had a real enlightening visit with your wife." Adam held back, his eyebrows raised in anticipation of Gavin's reaction.

Nothing.

"She proved *very* informative, let me tell you. Are you aware she wishes you had died too?"

Adam's words hit the mark. Gavin recoiled, then shrugged. "Understandable, I suppose, considering what I've put her and the girls through."

"Very noble of you, if you don't mind me saying."

Gavin shrugged one shoulder again. "It's true."

"Yes I agree, if you *were* guilty. But you're not, are you, Gavin? You know it, I know it and above all, your lovely wife knows it."

The next shrug wasn't as cocky. Gavin swallowed, staring at the table in front of him, his jaw clenching and unclenching.

"I worked out what caused your sudden confession."

A fake grin crossed Gavin's face as he fidgeted in his seat. "Is that so, Detective?"

Adam gave a slow nod and smiled back, one eyebrow raised.

"You see, what makes me a good detective, Gavin, is the fact I'm naturally intuitive. I know that regardless of all the evidence, you are no more capable of killing those men than I am."

Gavin shook his head. "Wrong, Detective. Your intuition might need to go into the shop for a service. I killed them," he sneered.

"However, for all that my senses tell me you're innocent, the opposite has to be said about your wife."

Gavin's jaw dropped and his breathing hitched.

Adam sat back in his chair, one arm stretched behind his head and the other strummed a beat on the table. He crossed his right foot over his left knee and sighed.

"Leave my wife out of this," Gavin growled. "She's been through enough."

It was Adam's turn to flippantly shrug one shoulder.

"I'm serious. I killed those men. Why the fuck won't you believe me?"

"Because you're lying, and I plan to prove you're covering for your wife," Adam said.

Gavin jumped up, sending his chair clattering to the concrete floor.

The prison officer leapt forwards, grabbed Gavin's upper arms and shoved him down.

Adam, now also on his feet, nodded. "Touch a nerve, did I?"

Gavin's face was pressed up against the floor, the officer's knee shoved in his back. "Leave Melissa alone!" he yelled. "I mean it, leave her be."

***

Mum wasted no time.

Certain the man was dead she yanked the knife free. It was much harder coming out than going in. Rummaging in the dead man's pockets, she pulled out his mobile phone and raced to the ladies. She washed the knife and her hands in the tiny sink.

Claude whimpered like a terrified baby, the poor thing was distraught. He cowered to the ground as Mum walked over to him. The manly growl from earlier was long gone.

She bent to undo his lead from the bench. "**Shut up, mutt!**" she spat, giving his lead a firm tug.

Mum, he's frightened.

"**So he bloody well should be.**"

Mum began running and Claude had no choice but to obey or be strung up by the neck.

She took a detour on the way home. I asked her what she intended to do, but she ignored me. We doubled back on ourselves, running along a few unknown streets before dropping Brett's phone into a storm-water drain.

Arriving home, it worried me Mum still had control. We raced into the kitchen. Mum dropped Claude's lead, threw the knife into the dishwasher and ran to the bedroom where she stripped off the anorak and the rest of the clothes.

Surprisingly, there wasn't any blood. Not visible to my bare eyes, anyway. On the CSI programme I used to watch, they use specialist lights to show up even the teeniest speck of blood, but I hoped there would be no cause for a CSI examination.

After putting on my gown, we headed back out to the kitchen where Tina and Stella fussed over Claude.

"Oh, there you are," Stella said. "We wondered what happened. We heard the back door slam and found Claude still attached to his lead and you no-where to be seen."

"Stop being so dramatic, Stella. I needed the toilet that's all."

"What happened to your clothes?" Stella eyed me.

"I removed them. I'm not sure what people do in France, but over here we remove our clothes before stepping into the shower," Mum said.

Tina and Stella glanced at each other and then back at Claude.

"Did something happen, Mum?" Stella asked, still fussing over the dog.

"No. Like what?"

She shrugged. "Claude's acting weird."

"Because he's the most unfit dog I've ever met. You girls ought to be ashamed of yourselves. He's a genuine canine couch potato."

In a way, I was relieved Mum still had control. Her sharp tongue would worry the girls, but I was more than happy to let things stay as they were for the time being. Without Mum, they would see straight through my act.

A tremor spread through my entire body. I'd just been party to a cold-blooded murder, one that I knew Mum had enjoyed. I'd sensed her unmistakable pleasure as the man drew his final breath.

Chapter 28

Stella burst through the back door and flung her keys and bag in the centre of the table in front of Tina, Yvonne and me.

"You'll never guess what?" Her eyes were almost bursting from the sockets.

"What?" We said in unison.

"A man was murdered in Parswood Park."

"For God's sake! This place is going to the dogs!" Yvonne screeched.

"Who?" Tina asked.

"Dunno. Mrs Greyson from the chippie told me. She said they have cordoned off the whole of Mambers Lane and the park. I'm going to check out the news." She rushed from the kitchen.

My heart raced. I couldn't say anything for fear of incriminating myself. They wouldn't suspect me, not in a million years, and I didn't intend to blurt out what I'd done, but still, I prayed for Mum's return.

Last night, she stayed with me until I drifted off to sleep. I spent the entire night in bed for the first time in weeks. This morning, the shocking enormity of what we'd done, hit me like a kick in the stomach, and there wasn't any sign of my mother.

"You all right, Mel?"

I almost jumped out of my skin as I noticed Tina standing over me, a slight frown on her face.

"Yeah, why?" I made a feeble attempt at a smile.

"You've gone pale. Are you ill?"

I shook my head. "Just tired." I ran my fingers through my hair, then got to my feet and began clearing the cups from the table. I placed them into the soapy dishwater in the sink.

After washing up, I retreated to my room and checked Gavin's phone, vaguely aware that Mum had made more arrangements with another man last night.

When she was in control it felt like a dream, and although I remembered everything that happened, the details afterwards were somewhat hazy.

Mum agreed we should leave brand new contacts alone, but anybody that Gavin had already met up with would need to be dealt with.

I located a message from *dirtidawg*, aka Merv. He'd suggested Gavin meet him at a hotel nearby, 7pm Friday evening. Mum replied, agreeing to meet up.

I knew the hotel in question. I'd been there to see a clairvoyant last year and from what I could remember, you needed to go through reception to get to the rooms, which might prove tricky.

We'd have to be extra careful.

***

The next morning, Adam found a report on his desk. Frances had gone through Melissa May's statement and found Melissa had no alibi at the time of each murder. Nobody had picked up on this earlier as she hadn't been a suspect.

Until now.

However, the case against her held no substance, and Adam didn't want to haul her in for questioning until he had something more concrete.

He had no doubts at all, she was the real killer. Nevertheless, with a signed confession from Gavin, he needed to be careful, or his bosses would haul him over the coals for wasting police time and resources on something a little more than a hunch.

He re-examined all the evidence and read the report on the computer records taken from the May's home. Nothing untoward showed up.

He went over all the original interviews with Gavin pleading his innocence. He explained about his first contact with the victims via a website designed for married, bi-sexual men.

It blew Adam's mind the kind of depravity available, courtesy of the Internet. In the past, these men would have struggled to find like-minded individuals. But nowadays, any fantasy or fetish was catered for and supported with one website or another, no matter how disgusting, depraved or sadistic.

What shocked him the most was the amount of people searching for, and dabbling in these kinds of activities.

Always choosing to be monogamous, Adam's sex life looked archaic and boring in comparison. He'd never entertain a one-night-stand. To him, the act of love-making was intimate and important and he needed a special connection to want to open himself up like that.

He knew this attitude was unheard of in this day and age, but he didn't care. Luckily Amanda seemed of the same mind. She did confess to a promiscuous episode, trying to find herself after all the sordid sexual acts she'd been subjected to as a child.

Now she was only interested in giving herself to one man wholeheartedly.

Thoughts of Amanda created a quickening sensation in his stomach. Normally, Sarah filled his every idle thought, which was why he tried to keep his mind busy. Now, when he got the chance, he found himself daydreaming about Amanda instead.

His heart sank as guilt enveloped him. He felt like he was betraying Sarah's memory, their marriage and the wonderful life they had shared. But he wasn't. He couldn't bring Sarah back and she wouldn't want him moping around for the rest of his life. She would have approved of Amanda, he was certain of that.

He planned to take Amanda and the children for a picnic on Saturday if the weather held up. Afterwards, Michael was to take Emma and Jacob for the night and Mary would stay at Sandra's. They would be free to do whatever they liked for the rest of the evening.

He only hoped he'd be closer to closing the case by then. He didn't want a repeat performance of last week, him being too distracted to relax and enjoy every second in her company.

He picked up the phone and hit one of the pre-programmed numbers. "Cal, I need you to get me a photograph."

He knocked at the door of the late Carl Pilkington. His widow opened the door. Adam could tell she'd been crying.

"Hi, Mrs Pilkington. Remember me?" He smiled, showing her his badge.

She nodded. "Yes, Detective, come on in." She beckoned for him to enter the tiny hallway and closed the door behind him. Then she awkwardly manoeuvred herself around him and opened the lounge door, leading him inside.

"What can I do for you, Detective?"

"I won't keep you long—I just have a couple of questions."

"Sit down." She gestured towards the sofa.

"Thanks." He took a seat.

"Can I get you anyfing? Tea? Coffee?"

"No, I'm good." He reached into his pocket and produced a photograph of Melissa May. "Can you tell me if you've ever seen this woman before?"

Sandy took the image from him and looked at it. Her eyebrows screwed together. "No, I don't fink so." Shaking her head, she handed the photo back to him.

"Are you sure, Sandy? This is important." Adam held the image towards her again.

She scrutinised it once more. "No, I don't know 'er, who is she? Is she connected to Carl's murder? I fought you'd already charged someone."

"We have. I'm just checking out another theory, that's all." He smiled, standing up to leave. "Oh well, never mind. Thanks anyway."

Next he called in to see Bethany Bates and showed her the photograph.

She too shook her head and handed it back to him. "No. Never seen her before."

Adam suspected she was highly medicated. He had first-hand knowledge of how that felt. He'd spent the first three months after Sarah, drugged to the eyeballs.

He sighed. "Okay, thank you, Mrs Bates."

He got the exact same reaction from Denise Stubbs, Joe Bates' receptionist, Mrs Kingsley, and the two witnesses who saw the silhouette of the cap-wearing person who mowed Anthony Kingsley down. No one had set eyes on Melissa May before.

His last stop, The Mirage Motel. The owner, Peter Lynch, was the man Adam had met the night they arrested Gavin May.

When Adam showed him the photograph, Peter recognised her right away. But Adam's initial excitement fell flat once he discovered she had called in to collect her husband's belongings *after* the murders.

Today had proved a complete waste of his time.

On his way back to the station, Adam's car phone rang.

"Stanley."

"Detective, it's Peter Lynch from The Mirage."

"Yes, Mr Lynch. What can I do for you?"

"I wanted to check that Mrs May gave you the mobile phone we found in her husband's unit. I told her I intended to hand it in to you guys, but she insisted she did it instead."

"Very interesting, and no she didn't hand it in. Thanks for that, I'll chase it up."

Chapter 29

Yvonne had agreed to go home. I followed her up-stairs to help pack her belongings before Keith arrived, when the phone rang.

"Mum, phone," Stella yelled.

I made my way down the stairs.

Stella stood in the hallway, the phone held to her breast. "A Detective Stanley."

My stomach dropped to the floor as a white light settled all around me, accompanied by the familiar, awful noise.

Stella's mouth opened and closed, but I couldn't hear a word she said. She dropped the phone and gripped both my shoulders, shaking me roughly.

All of a sudden, Mum returned.

"**What? Get off me**." She lifted both arms, shoving Stella away from her.

"Are you okay?"

"**Course I'm okay**." Mum shook her head, before reaching for the dangling phone.

"**Yes, Detective?**"

"Mrs May, is this a bad time?"

"**Not at all. What can I do for you**?"

"I believe you have your husband's mobile phone."

"**No. I don't**."

"Are you sure?"

"**The motel manager told me he intended to pass it on to you**."

"Strange. He said you took it."

"**Certainly not!**"

"I see. That will be all for now then, Mrs May."

Mum hung up, noticing Stella still hovering behind her.

"What did he want?" she asked.

"**He's looking for Dad's phone**."

"Then, why lie?"

"**I didn't. I don't have it!**" Mum glared at Stella.

"You do. Dad's phone is in your bedroom."

Mum, walking towards the kitchen, stopped and spun around to face Stella, fuming. "**Keep your fucking nosey beak out of my business. I'm sick of the lot of you snooping into things of no concern to you**."

"Sorry, Mum, I ..."

"**Sorry, Mum—Sorry, Mum**." She mimicked. "**Change the fucking record will you?**"

"Mother!" Yvonne said racing down the stairs.

A rapping at the door made everyone stop in their tracks. Yvonne opened the door and Keith stepped inside pulling his wife into his arms.

"Hey, baby, what's the matter?" he asked.

"Just take me home, Keith." She sobbed into his neck.

Mum scowled at her and continued to the kitchen where Claude began to whimper.

"You can fuck off and all! You stinking mutt."

Tina, sitting at the dining table, had witnessed everything. She jumped to her feet. "Hey, don't be like that, Mel." Her voice quivered.

"You don't like it? You know where the door is."

"Fine! Come on, Stella. Nobody needs to put up with this abuse."

Within half an hour everyone had gone, including Mum.

I sat on my bed feeling sorry for myself. Not sad they'd gone, I wouldn't miss any of them. Well, maybe Claude, I'd grown quite fond of him. It was how it all came about that upset me. Apart from the odd spat, I'd never had an argument with my girls.

I stayed in my room until the sun had gone down, and I found myself sitting in darkness.

I heated a bowl of soup for dinner, I went through to the lounge and turned on the TV.

I'd watched very little TV the past few weeks. The noise that accompanied it seemed to drive me demented, but the quiet of the house after everyone being there also disturbed me.

I muted the sound and flicked through a few channels but nothing caught my eye until I stumbled upon a photo of Brett, the guy from the park.

I turned on the sound and listened to what the newsreader had to say.

... Police have ruled out robbery as a motive because Mr Graham's wallet and other valuables were found on his person. The only item that appears to be missing, at this stage, is his cell phone.

What Mr Graham was doing in the park is still a mystery, although CCTV footage from the car park shows he arrived of his own volition.

Surrey Police appeal for any witnesses to come forward. Even the smallest piece of information could make all the difference ...

I muted the TV. My whole body trembled. I'd not even considered there might be CCTV cameras operating in the area. And depending on where they were positioned, Claude and I could well have been picked up by them too.

How could I have been so stupid to allow Mum to do this?

***

Adam hung up the phone and scratched his head. Now why would she lie about having Gavin's phone? There must be something she didn't want him to see.

Gavin told him he accessed the website via his phone, one of the reasons he wanted to get his hands on it. But there was more than one way to skin a cat, as his Mum used to say.

Kimberley Owens was Adam's favourite computer geek. He gave her the website details he'd got from Gavin days ago, and left it with her.

She said she'd leave the findings on his desk by morning.

On his way home, he picked up a Chinese takeaway, looking forward to an early night.

Halfway through his meal, the phone rang.

"Adam, I think you may want to get back here. I've got something to show you." Kimberley's voice was breathy and excited.

Twenty minutes later Adam strode into Kimberley's office.

"You were quick," she said.

"It sounded urgent."

"It is. Here, grab a seat and look at this." She turned the computer screen in his direction.

Adam shuffled his chair up beside her.

"I got into Gavin's profile."

"Aha." Adam nodded, eager to get to the reason she'd called him back.

"Well, Gavin met up with hundreds of guys on here, including the first two murder victims."

"Okay."

"Dozens of messages in the past few weeks have gone unanswered."

"Of course, Gavin's locked up."

"I know. Which is why I thought it odd he'd arranged to meet a man a couple of nights ago. At a park." Kimberley glanced at him. "In Surrey." Her eyes widened, as if waiting for the penny to drop.

Adam shook his head. "What am I not getting? Firstly, Gavin couldn't have arranged the meeting and secondly, why are you looking at me like that?"

"Don't you listen to the news, Detective?"

"When I get a chance. Why?"

She pulled up an image of a middle aged man. "This man, Brett Graham, arranged to meet Gavin in Parswood Park in Surrey at 7pm last Tuesday."

"Yeah, you said."

"This same man was found outside the toilets in Parswood Park at 7.45pm on Tuesday. He'd been stabbed to death."

Chapter 30

I woke up in the same position on the sofa. It was morning already, considering the sounds made by the bird community who were going about their business outside the window.

I loved having the house to myself again, although I still worried about the argument I'd had with the girls.

They'll live.

"Oh, hello. I thought you'd bailed on me too."

No chance of that. We've got work to do.

"I don't know. Can't we just—?"

For the last time, these men need to be stopped. Especially the ones we know are spreading their disease.

I couldn't argue with her. She gave me a headache.

I'll do everything. You're not much help anyway. Never was.

"Stop being nasty, Mother. I don't think I've done so bad considering the start in life you provided."

Go on, same old broken record.

I shook my head. "Just leave me alone."

My pleasure, but first we need to do some research for tonight.

"What research?"

You'll see.

"Go! You're spoiling my peace and quiet."

I stomped into the bathroom, slammed the door behind me and turned on the shower. After stripping off my clothes, I stepped underneath the hot jets, closing my eyes as the soothing water pummelled my exhausted body.

This was the perfect time to cry, and I knew I should want to, but I didn't. It was as though a layer of cotton wool had been wrapped around my feelings, buffering my emotions and reactions.

Afterwards, I felt much better. For the first time in ages I applied some moisturiser, followed by eyeliner and a dab of lipstick which seemed to lift my face *and* my mood.

I smiled at my reflection in the mirror and suddenly Mum's face appeared in front of my own. Although similar, her eyes had a hardness to them, and her lips formed a tight firm line.

"I thought you'd gone."

You'll never get rid of me, girl. Don't you forget that.

Her image faded and I was left staring at my own face once again.

Going through to the bedroom, I threw on a shirt and pair of slacks.

After coffee and a slice of toast, I was ready. "Right, Mother. What is your plan?"

The hotel had a huge conference room off the reception area where the clairvoyant had performed.

I approached the main desk and it seemed to take all the young, blonde girl's energy to tear her eyes away from the computer screen in front of her. I guessed she was in the middle of an on-line game or chatting with her friends on Facebook.

"How can I help you?" She glanced up, feigning interest. Her mouth was pursed as though I was an inconvenience.

"I have some friends coming to town next week, and they'll need somewhere to stay. I wondered if I could have some information about what you offer?"

"Yes, no problem." She glanced back at the screen and clicked the mouse a few times before standing up and picking a glossy coloured brochure up from a pile. "We have standard rooms, superior rooms and executive rooms. The main difference in these is the size of the bed—standard has a double, superior, a queen and executive, a king," she said, pointing to each of the pictures with a pen, her voice reminiscent of a recording. She'd clearly memorised the spiel word for word.

I nodded and smiled.

"All our rooms include a full English breakfast in our Quartz restaurant, and a full a la carte menu is available for dinner. We also offer a twenty-four hour room service menu."

As she spoke I let my eyes wander around the room, glancing back at her with a smile. A camera faced the double front doors and another faced the reception desk. There would be no way of entering without being picked up by both of them.

"Any chance of looking at the rooms?"

"We don't have any spare staff to show you around at the moment, but I can give you a couple of room keys if you don't mind?"

"No, not at all." I offered her my sweetest smile.

She swiped two cards into a machine and punched in some numbers then handed them to me.

"Room 803 is a standard and 620 is an executive, which should give you a good idea."

"Lovely, thanks for that."

At the end of the first corridor was a sign for the car park. The door opened freely to exit, but needed a swipe card to enter. Another camera pointed at the door from the outside. I dragged a rubbish bin from the corridor and wedged it to prevent the door from closing while I went to check out the rest of the car park.

I scanned the entire area and only found one other camera positioned to catch anybody coming in via the ramp from outside.

I nodded, satisfied I'd found them all and scooted back into the corridor, putting the rubbish bin back where I'd found it. I didn't need to view the rooms but was unsure if the girl would be able to tell, so I located each room and spent a moment inside both.

Back in the reception, I placed the cards on the desk in front of the blond girl, who now chatted on the phone.

She nodded and smiled at me.

I gave her the thumbs up and left.

"Bugger!" I said as I climbed into my car.

Don't worry, I have a plan.

"No way, Mum. There are cameras all over the place—it's impossible."

There's no such thing as impossible—just different degrees of difficult.

***

Dressed in the same dark clothing as Tuesday, Mum took control.

She drove to the hotel and parked a few minutes' walk away, down a side street.

Pulling on the hood of the anorak, Mum tightened the cord ties, fitting it around my face.

We'd received a text message earlier from Merv, the man we were due to meet, telling Gavin he was in room 201.

Mum checked the phone for any more messages. Nothing. She slipped it back into the pocket and patted her sleeve to check the position of the knife before getting out of the car.

We walked along the back streets, approaching the hotel from the rear.

The car park entrance had a barrier arm that was operated using a swipe card. Mum approached the barrier, keeping her back to the camera and ducked underneath. Stepping into the shadows to the side of the wall, she waited to see if she'd triggered any alarms. Nothing happened.

The air stank of car fumes, a mixture of old motor oil and petrol.

Mum walked the perimeter of the car park until reaching the two hundreds, pleased to find a white Hyundai parked up in 201.

She approached the car and scanned the area one last time, and slid the knife from her sleeve. She leaned against the driver's side of the car, placing the handle end of the knife against the side window. With one last glance around, she whacked the glass with the handle.

The deafening crack echoed off every wall in the enclosed space. Yet Mum, unperturbed, continued.

It took several attempts before the window shattered, showering thousands of tiny glass beads all over the seat.

Mum sought out the shadows once again and waited, hardly breathing.

Once satisfied nobody had been alerted, Mum took Gavin's phone from my pocket and dialled a number she had entered earlier.

"Swainston Manor, Trudy speaking. How may I help you?"

"Room 201, please."

"Of course, madam."

After a brief pause and two long rings reminding me of an overseas call, the phone clicked.

"Hello?" A deep male voice said.

"Reception desk here, sir. It seems security have reported a broken window on a vehicle parked in the car park bay allocated to your room. They need you to meet them at the car."

"What? Oh shit, I'll be right there."

Mum positioned herself behind the vehicle next to Merv's and crouched down as she watched the internal door.

Within a few minutes, a tall man appeared wearing a heavy grey overcoat. He headed straight for the car, then stopped, his hands on his hips, shaking his head.

Once again, Mum slid the knife from her sleeve, and, still bending, crept up behind the man. She raised the knife past her shoulder, preparing to put all our weight behind that first thrust.

All of a sudden, floodlights lit the whole car park.

The surprise gripped Mum to the core.

The man turned to face her, smiling.

The shock was immense. I struggled to work out what the hell had just happened.

"Hello, Melissa," Detective Stanley said.

Chapter 31

Adam pulled his car into the traffic and followed the police van to the Surrey station.

"Are you okay?" He glanced at Frances, who seemed spaced out, in the passenger seat.

"I'm fine." She gave him an unconvincing smile.

"You're not hurt?"

She shook her head. "No. Honestly, I'm fine."

Adam shrugged.

It had been all systems go since last night. After contacting the Surrey station, they'd joined forces in order to catch Melissa red-handed. The only hitch had been Merv the Perv, as they'd all christened him, who refused to help them at first, petrified his wife would find out what he'd been up to. Adam promised total discretion and he eventually agreed to cooperate.

The hotel provided two adjoining rooms for their use. The Surrey police set up cameras and one of their detectives planned to play the part of Merv.

However, earlier today, Adam almost bumped straight into Melissa, which would have blown the whole thing. Luckily, she didn't see him. Adam managed to dart back into the room, slamming the door in time, but it shook him up. They had been so close to ruining everything.

He never even considered Melissa might check the place out first, and that hadn't been the only mistake. All their hard work went tits up when Melissa tried to trick Merv out of the room.

Adam refused to allow their Merv substitute to go down to the car park. If any risks were to be taken, he would be the one to take them. So he donned the overcoat, pulling the collar up tight around his face and made the call to go down himself.

Time seemed to stop the moment he turned around.

Melissa froze, arm raised and eyes wide open.

Adam watched the confusion and then the realisation dawn on her.

The disbelief rendered her speechless and her mouth opened and closed wordlessly.

Moments later all hell broke loose.

Frances came out of nowhere, pouncing on Melissa from behind, wrestling the knife from her hand. They both crashed to the floor, sending the knife skittering across the concrete and underneath Merv's car.

Within seconds, they were surrounded by at least a dozen detectives. They picked Melissa up, restraining her before reading her her rights. She was then bundled, kicking and screaming, into the back of a police van which was headed for the Surrey station.

Adam made it clear to the other officers that he had first dibs on her. There was no way he would let them get to her first.

At the station, Melissa was taken to be booked in.

Adam took Frances for a bite to eat. No doubt it would be a long night once they began the questioning.

The canteen was typical of any police canteen he'd ever been in. The basic food and drinks were better than nothing, marginally. Frances ordered a Jacket potato filled with beans and cheese. Adam chose liver and onions with mashed potato and gravy. His stomach growled in anticipation.

They sat down with a cup of coffee while waiting for their food.

"You seem distracted. What's wrong?" Adam asked.

"Just thinking, about how I accused you of being crazy when you suggested Gavin could be innocent."

"I know you did, but that's all right. You're not the first and won't be the last." Adam smiled and leaned back in his chair, glancing round. He was starving.

"Doesn't make me a very good detective though, does it?"

"You're a great detective, you fool." Adam touched her hand and shook his head.

"But you're obviously better."

"Obviously." He laughed.

Frances joined in, giving him a playful nudge.

They found Melissa in the interview room when they got back from the canteen.

Gone, the timid, slight woman they'd met at her home. Instead, she almost filled the room with her indignant attitude. He glanced at Frances and realised she'd noticed the change too. He took a seat opposite Melissa.

Frances sat next to him and stated their names, date and time into the recorder.

"Melissa, I want to confirm you were read your rights and if so, understood them," Adam said.

Melissa sneered at him, her nose screwed as though he was a stinky hunk of shit on her shoe.

"Mrs May?"

"Wrong name, I'm not *his* wife."

"Sorry, my mistake. Gavin told us you were married." Adam glanced at Frances again. "So what would you prefer we call you, then?"

"Maureen will do."

"Maureen? What about Melissa?" Adam asked.

"I already told you, my name's Maureen."

"I'm confused. Please explain. Where is Melissa?"

She stared at him, her eyes filled with defiance. She said nothing.

"At our last meeting, you said your name was Melissa May?"

"No, I didn't, Melissa did."

"Are you her sister? Her twin perhaps?"

The sneer deepened. "Don't be so stupid," she spat. "I'm her mother."

Once again, Adam glanced at Frances, who looked as confused as he felt.

"Do you know why you're here, Maureen?"
She nodded.

"Please speak up for the tape," Frances said.

"Yes. Of course I do. Because I tried to kill you."

"Not forgetting the other murders, including the ones your husb ... er, Gavin confessed to."

"This is all his doing, if he'd kept his dick in his pants none of this would have happened."

"You killed the victims because Gavin slept with them?"

She nodded. "Yes. For spreading his disease. He's already infected my daughter and Lord knows how many other innocent people, but that wasn't enough for him."

"I get you. You wanted to stop these men infecting their wives, but what about the man you killed in the park and the one you intended to kill tonight? They didn't sleep with Gavin." Adam shook his head.

"He'd already slept with them, many times. Do you know how many bisexual men are married with children? Gavin's phone is filled with hundreds of them. They live a lie and spread their disgusting, contaminated seed."

"Where does Melissa fit into all this?" Frances asked.

"Melissa, bah! She's useless. I told her to kill her putrid husband when she had the chance."

"Why didn't she?"

Maureen's face screwed up. "Because she *loved him,*" she said.

"Maybe you need to tell us the whole story, from the beginning. What happened?"

After Melissa's full and frank confession, Adam was clueless as to where the hell they stood. It was obvious Melissa May, or Maureen Clark as she called herself, had lost her grip on reality. She needed a psychiatric evaluation, and it may well turn out her confession wouldn't be worth the paper it was written on.

They drove back to London in the early hours of Saturday morning, exhausted and ready for bed. Adam still had a mountain of paperwork to get through before knocking off. Frances slept most of the journey, and Adam insisted she go home for a well-deserved rest.

He sat down at his desk, relieved to finally prove Gavin's innocence after all. Well, partial innocence. Gavin was guilty of having unprotected sex knowing his HIV status, and showed no remorse.

In a way, he applauded Melissa. In her own befuddled mind she had been protecting other innocent people, although he couldn't condone the way she'd gone about it.

Anthony Kingsley had been a tragic mistake. The poor guy had been in the wrong place at the wrong time. If he hadn't forgotten the paperwork, he'd never have gone back to Gavin's unit. Instead, he would still be enjoying life with his wife and twins.

But that was the problem with crime. Breaking the law, albeit with good intentions, inevitably escalates out of control. Lies create more lies—deceit more deceit.

In Melissa's case, Carl Pilkington's accidental death had managed to flip her over the edge mentally.

Chapter 32

Driving home, Adam was greeted by the most amazing sunrise. He squinted as he watched the blinding orange sphere rise from the horizon taking its place in the cloudless blue sky.

He smiled. A perfect day for a picnic.

He'd arranged to pick up Amanda and the children at 11.30am, which would give him plenty of time to get his head down for a couple of hours.

He'd pre-ordered a picnic hamper from the local deli, ensuring there would be a variety of foods and goodies for the children.

Being new to London, he hadn't a clue where to take a young family for a day out. Amanda chose the location, Clapham Common.

Thankfully, he would be able to focus on the day, now Melissa was off the streets.

He slid between the sheets and glanced at the clock—5.43am. Setting the alarm for 10am, would give him four hours sleep and time to shower, pick up the picnic hamper and get to Amanda's on time.

***

Amanda opened her eyes and sprang out of bed in one fluid movement, and raced down the hallway. She dropped to the bathroom floor and skidded the last few inches on her knees, projectile vomiting into the bowl.

After a few minutes of retching, she rolled onto her bottom and reached for a towel to wipe her mouth.

The thumping of tiny feet along the hallway told her at least one of the children was up. With a final glance at the toilet bowl, she got to her feet and went in search of the children.

Jacob sat in the middle of his tiny bedroom, bottom in the air, head on the street mat. He made a *brrruu-ummmm*-ing sound as he pushed a car along the road.

"Good morning, Jaky. You're up early." Amanda crouched beside her youngest child.

At almost two years old, Jacob happily lived in his sister's shadow. However, his own personality was beginning to emerge and he was obsessed with cars. He'd recently made the transition from cot to bed and after a few teething problems, had settled down well.

Jacob loved his sleep, and this was the first time he'd woken before Emma. Amanda relished the few moments they had alone.

"What have you got there, Jaky?"

"Car." He held it up for her inspection.

"Ooh, that's a flash, blue car. Look at those yellow stripes."

"Stipes." He inspected the car, placing one pudgy finger along the stripe.

"Yes, that's right, baby. Stripes."

Amanda groaned and rubbed her stomach, tipping her head back as a sigh escaped. What the hell was wrong with her? She must have eaten something dodgy.

"Mummy, Mummy, Mummy."

Emma broke the peace and quiet as she ran from her room.

"In here, Em."

She burst into the room, a mass of blonde curls and pink pyjamas. "Are we going yet?"

"Going where?"

"Our picanic."

Amanda groaned again. If her stomach didn't settle, they wouldn't be going anywhere. "Not for ages yet. You need your breakfast first."

"Yay! Chuckie eggs?"

Sandra had got them into eating boiled eggs, mashed in a cup, with toast soldiers.

"I suppose. Would you like eggs too, Jaky?"

Jacob nodded as he rummaged through his up-turned toy-box.

"Okeydokey, let's change your nappy first then, mister."

Potty training was to be their next mission.

A couple of hours later Amanda was still feeling queasy, although, not as bad. She couldn't understand it. She'd eaten nothing out of the ordinary and the kids were fine, which probably ruled out a stomach bug. The last time she felt like this was …

She gasped.

Placing her hands on either side of her on the sofa, she froze for a moment then leapt to her feet, racing to the kitchen.

A calendar the kids had made at day-care hung on the fridge door. She trailed a finger down the dates and gasped again.

"No …" she shook her head.

"No. I can't be …"

Dazed, she sat down at the table. Her throat had thickened and she struggled to swallow.

It didn't make sense—they'd been careful. She suddenly remembered a broken condom and she froze. This was all she needed.

Adam was due within the hour. How would she be able look at him now? Maybe she should cancel. But he would have gone to a lot of trouble to prepare a picnic for them all. She couldn't do that to him. No— she'd have to just go along with it.

The children were playing in Emma's bedroom and were having a wonderful time if the bumps and laughter were anything to go by.

Mary was in the bathroom getting ready.

Rummaging around in the fridge drawer, Amanda found a hunk of ginger, the only thing that managed to settle her stomach during her last two pregnancies. She proceeded to grate the ginger to make a tea.

By the time Adam arrived, she felt almost human again.

"Are you okay? You look a little peaky." Adam pulled her into his arms in the small hallway, burying his face in her neck.

"Think I might be sickening for something. Don't get too close."

"I don't mind sharing your germs." He smiled. "Are you ready?"

"Yes. The kids have been ready for hours." She laughed. "Adam's here. Come on, you lot," she called up the stairs.

Mary appeared at the top of the stairs. "Hi, Adam." She smiled, before suddenly being pushed aside by two tearaways.

"Calm down, calm down. Someone will get hurt." Amanda took a few steps and grabbed both children by the arms, escorting them down the final steps.

"Are we going on a picanic now?" Emma squealed.

"We sure are, kiddo." Adam ruffled her hair.

"A picanic," Jacob babbled.

"Yes, Jacob. A picanic—picnic." He laughed. "They've got me at it now."

Chapter 33

Gavin was glad to be back in his own clothes.

The prison guard opened an envelope and asked him to sign for the contents—his watch, wedding ring and a handful of loose change. He wouldn't get far on £5.65p. His house key wasn't even there.

He didn't care, all he needed was to get out of there as soon as possible, and he'd deal with the rest later.

The guard escorted Gavin through several security gates until he stepped out onto the street. As the final gate closed behind him, he sighed, leaning against the stone wall of the prison, while he tried to catch his breath and think about his next move.

He turned at the sound of footsteps running towards him.

"Dad!" Yvonne cried as she launched herself into his arms.

"Hey, hey." He held his arms out to the side, before slowly wrapping them around his daughter.

He hadn't been sure what his reception would be, but he hadn't expected this.

Keith crossed over the road in front of them.

Gavin nodded a greeting.

Keith's smile was tight-lipped.

That's more like it, Gavin thought.

"You're so thin, Dad. Are you okay?" Yvonne asked.

"I'll be better when I get home. Do you have a door key?"

"I do, and I bought groceries. We stayed at yours last night."

They began walking—shuffling really. Yvonne held him so tight he struggled to move any faster. Keith led the way to the car.

"Have you seen your mother?"

"They won't allow visitors, but they're saying she's lost her mind. She's been sectioned."

He nodded.

"I told Keith she wasn't right in the head, didn't I, Keith?"

Keith nodded.

"But I didn't think she'd be capable of murder. Did you?" Yvonne jabbered on.

Gavin sighed, before nodding once again. "I guessed."

"Is that the reason you confessed?"

He shrugged. "I didn't want her in trouble. My actions drove her to it, after all."

They reached the car and Yvonne jumped into the back seat leaving Gavin to sit in the front beside Keith, who hadn't even looked at him since that first semi-smile. Keith buckled his belt and started the car.

"I've been researching your condition." Yvonne continued. "They're making massive inroads lately. I'm sure it won't be long before they find a cure."

Gavin faced forward, not responding. Fuck—he'd just got out of prison. What he needed was a full English breakfast and a pot of tea, not a full and frank discussion about HIV—especially not with his eldest daughter and her toffee-nosed, opinionated husband.

However, Yvonne wasn't deterred.

"Yes. They've had some sort of breakthrough with a drug combination. I can't remember what, but I intend to find out all about it for you."

"That's nice." He nodded.

"Stella and Tina are on their way back too. They'll be able to help you with the other thing, you know, the gay thing."

"Whoa, back the bus up. I'm not gay."

"Bisexual then—same difference."

"It is not!" he said, fear clutching his gut. He thought the worst thing was being in prison. How would he cope with everyone knowing his secret?

He already missed the seclusion of his prison cell.

Chapter 34

All bundled into the car, the kids chattering ten-to-the dozen, Adam glanced at Amanda.

She certainly wasn't her normal self. Not only because of the way she looked, but the stiff way she held herself and the troubled expression in her eyes.

His first thought was Andrew.

If Andrew had been in touch, Adam would be the last person she'd confide in.

She caught his glance and smiled at him, sighing deeply.

You okay? He mouthed.

She nodded, the smile still fixed in place.

The park heaved with families, seemingly with the same intention. They walked for fifteen minutes until they reached the bandstand in the centre of the park.

"Here okay?" Adam asked, dropping the bags and taking the French loaf from under his arm.

Amanda shrugged. "Good a place as any."

"You sure?" He knew she didn't like crowds, but she seemed to be coping all right.

"Sure." She shook out the blanket and straightened the corners on the grass.

Adam prayed the children would like the food. He'd ordered a mixed hamper. He wasn't disappointed. They had chicken nibbles, cold meats, pork pie, cocktail sausages, pasta salad, coleslaw, ready-made sandwiches, watermelon and strawberries. Plus two bottles of sparkling grape juice.

"Wow!" Amanda said as she sat down beside him.

Adam smiled. "I did good?"

"You did flippin' brilliant."

"I want ice-cream," Jacob said.

"You would, mister. Eat some lunch first." She handed him a sausage.

He popped the whole thing into his mouth.

Emma laughed and did the same.

"Emma, use your manners, please." Amanda shook her head and rolled her eyes at Adam.

Mary handed them each a paper plate.

Afterwards, Emma and Jacob chased each other around the bandstand. Mary stayed close by watching they didn't venture too far.

"That was delicious, thank you," Amanda said.

"Confession time."

She raised her eyebrows. "Go on."

"I didn't make it. I bought it ready made." He braced himself, a small smile playing on his lips.

"I know that already."

"How?" His shoulders fell.

"Der ... every item had a sticker underneath saying *Coles Deli*."

"So I didn't convince you for a minute?"

"Not for a second." She laughed. "But that doesn't mean I wasn't impressed all the same."

"You didn't eat much."

"Got a funny tummy today. Sorry."

"We could have postponed till another day."

"Then what would you have done with all this food?"

"You have a point. I would probably have taken it into the station—that horrible lot would have devoured it in seconds."

"Anyway, I enjoyed myself—I enjoy spending time with you.

"Me too." He squeezed her hand, wanting nothing more than to pull her into his arms and taste those juicy pink lips of hers. But she didn't want any displays of affection in front of the children, which was fair enough. They'd have the whole evening together.

"So tell me how you're getting on with your case."

"All solved." He shrugged one nonchalant shoulder.

"Solved?" She squeaked. "And?"

"Like I said—he was innocent."

"You're joking. So ... who?"

"I shouldn't say, really, but I'm sure the media will know the whole story by now. The killer was his wife."

"His wife?" she repeated, her mouth agape. "Why?"

"You need to ask google if you want any more." He laughed.

"Aw! Tell me."

He heaved a sigh. "Let's just say her motives were admirable. However, her actions weren't."

"Like Andrew?" Her blue eyes saddened.

"I guess." He nodded and squeezed her hand once again.

"Can we get an ice-cream now, Mummy?" Emma huffed, bending over beside them to catch her breath, her hands on her knees.

Mary approached with Jacob in her arms. She looked as though she might snap in half with the sheer weight of him.

"Tell you what, Amanda," Adam said, getting to his feet. "You take them for ice-cream and I'll get this little lot back to the car, then we can go for a walk. There's supposed to be a pond here somewhere."

***

With Jacob back in his pushchair, they ordered three ice-creams and found a bench to wait for Adam.

Mary seemed more reserved than usual and her ice-cream was fast-melting down her arm.

"Getting in a mess there, honey?" Amanda laughed.

Mary smiled and held the ice-cream out to Amanda. "Do you want some?"

"No, thanks, I'm stuffed. Have you had enough?"

She sighed and nodded, licking the melted ice-cream from her fingers.

"Here, hang on." Amanda stood and took the cone from her, then dropped it into the almost overflowing rubbish bin. With her other hand, she rummaged in her handbag for a tissue. "Here you go, love."

Mary took the tissue and wiped her mouth.

"Something wrong?"

Their eyes met and Mary's fell back to her sticky fingers. She shook her head.

"Are you sure? You know you can talk to me about anything, don't you?"

She nodded. Taking a deep breath she held it for a few seconds as though contemplating something.

Amanda sat beside her once again, torn between wanting to clean Jacob, who was in a fair old mess, and encouraging Mary to confide in her. Jacob would have to wait. Emma was sitting on the concrete path at his feet and they were busy entertaining each other.

"I saw you holding hands with Adam. Is he your boyfriend?"

"Kinda." Amanda smiled. "Why? Don't you like him?"

"I like him, but …"

"Go on, you're okay." Amanda nodded.

"If you marry him, what will happen to me?"

Mary gave a series of sniffs and tears filled her pretty blue eyes, breaking Amanda's heart.

"Oh, come here, silly." She pulled Mary into her arms. "You'll always be a part of this family, whatever happens. You hear me?"

Amanda hated the fact Mary still felt unsettled. She'd tried her best to make her welcome, but it obviously wasn't enough. The death of her mother, as well as her father's disappearance, affected her badly. Amanda wished she could tell her the whole truth, one that Andrew had confessed to her before he vanished. Mary was actually Amanda's child, born of incest and years of abuse. After she was born, she was immediately given up for adoption. Andrew and Judy, his wife, had brought her up as their own, after Andrew had kidnapped her from her adoptive family when she was just a small child.

But she couldn't tell her. How would Mary ever understand, or even get over the fact her aunt is actually her mother. And the only father she'd ever known is definitely her uncle, but also he had a one in two chance of being her real father—along with her grandfather.

Mary was already damaged, feeling abandoned and rejected. This information could well tip her over the edge.

Amanda's other problem was one more unplanned pregnancy, if her instinct was correct, which would have to be dealt with. How could she bring another child into such a disjointed and fucked up family as hers? Not only that, her relationship with Adam was much too new to be able to cope.

"There you are."

Adam's voice shocked her back to the present.

"Did you enjoy your ice-cream? Jacob, you look like you got more on you than in your mouth." He laughed.

Amanda jumped up and produced another wad of tissues from her bag. She handed Emma a couple before tackling her son's sticky mess.

"You okay, Mary?" Adam asked, raising his eyebrows at Amanda.

Amanda shrugged one shoulder and shook her head slightly.

"Yes, thanks," Mary said.

"Great. Are we all ready to feed the ducks?" Adam held up a loaf of bread.

"Yay!" Emma and Jacob squealed in unison.

"You thought of everything," Amanda said.

"Don't sound so amazed. It's always been a dream of mine—picnic in the park with a wonderful family, all playing Frisbee afterwards."

"You don't have a Frisbee?" Amanda said, looking at his other hand.

"I do, but I left it in the car." He laughed again.

Amanda shook her head, amazed. This guy seemed too good to be true. She stroked her flat stomach. He would make a perfect father, but the timing was way off.

They set off in search of the duck pond.

Jacob, sick of being in his pushchair, ran beside them but struggled to keep up, so Adam twirled him up onto his shoulders. He then ran on ahead with Emma chasing them both. Hysterical laughter came from their direction.

Amanda and Mary walked behind, linking arms and pushing the pushchair between them.

Mary chuckled as she watched the others.

Amanda hugged her arm. "Do you like being part of this family, Mary?"

Big blue eyes looked up at her with inherited dark smudges underneath. "Yes, I love it."

"And we love you too. Always will. Whoever else comes along, whatever else changes, that will always remain the same. I couldn't imagine my life without you now."

Mary inhaled sharply then smiled. "Me too."

Chapter 35

After a great day, all three children fell asleep in the car.

Amanda had arranged to drop them off at Sandra's and Michael would pick Emma and Jacob up from there. Sandra and Mary planned to go to the cinema and for a burger supper.

Adam couldn't wait to get his hands on Amanda—it had been torture all day.

They barely made it through the front door before they were groping and tearing at each other's clothes.

They made love on the stairs and afterwards, Adam carried her to the bedroom where he gave an encore performance—this time much slower and controlled.

He gazed at her sleeping, her head on his chest—blonde hair fanned out beneath her, long eyelashes flickering, her cheeks more drawn and pinched than usual. His breath hitched at her unassuming beauty. This woman was well and truly under his skin.

They both slept, waking a couple of hours later to make love once again.

"I'm starving," Amanda said afterwards, settling into the crook of his arm.

"I could go get the last of the picnic from the car."

Amanda shuddered. "No thanks, it's been in the hot car all day."

"Oh yeah. Do you fancy Chinese?"

"Oooh, I'd love some Chicken Chow Mein."

"Your wish is my command, little lady." He kissed the tip of her button nose before hopping from the bed and throwing on his jeans and t-shirt.

"Hmm, you going commando?" She giggled, chucking his white cotton boxers his way.

"Less for you to remove when I get back." He lay beside her again on top of the duvet and groaned. "You sure you need food?" He nuzzled at her throat.

"Afraid so, stud. You can't wear me out like that without sustenance." She shrugged away from him.

"Spoilsport." He groaned again and got to his feet. "Keep the bed warm. I'll be right back."

Twenty minutes later, he stepped from the car, his arms laden with delicious smelling brown paper bags. He kicked the door shut and awkwardly hit the lock button on the key-ring.

There was a stillness in the air as the last of the day's sunshine fell away. Stepping onto the garden path, Adam was startled by a movement to the side of him.

A dark clothed figure took to his heels, heading for the path at the side of the house.

Adam dropped the bags and gave chase.

"Hey!" he yelled. "Police. Stop."

The assailant crashed into the wheelie bin at the side of the house, sending it flying. A mixture of good-luck and nifty footwork prevented him crashing to the concrete too, but he'd been slowed down sufficiently.

Adam launched himself bodily, landing on top of the man and forcefully turning him onto his back. With one hand he held the guy's two wrists above his head, with the other he pulled off the black woollen hat.

The back door opened and Adam turned to see Amanda standing in the doorway, still fastening the tie of her silky robe. She stifled a scream, raising her hands to her mouth.

Adam closed his eyes and sighed before re-focusing.

"Andrew Kidd. I'm arresting you for the murders of Dennis Kidd, Annie Duncan and Brian Crosby ...

The End

ABOUT THE AUTHOR

Netta Newbound, originally from Manchester, England, now lives in New Zealand with her husband, Paul and their boxer dog Alfie. She has three grown-up children and two delicious grandchildren.

For more information or just to touch base with Netta you will find her at:
www.nettanewbound.com
Facebook
Twitter

Please don't forget to leave a review at your Amazon store.

Acknowledgements

Massive thanks to my family—especially my husband Paul for all your support and encouragement.

To my wonderful critique partners Sandra Toornstra, Linda Dawley, Serena Amadis and Jono Newbound—you're the best.

To my Editor, proof reader and friend Sandra Toornstra. You're amazing.

And finally, to the BOCHOK Babes – my go-to group for anything from critiquing to formatting or just a good old moan. Where would I be without you?

Printed in Great Britain
by Amazon